WAS LOVE THE BEST MEDICINE?

His kisses were unequivocal. This was a man who knew what he wanted, and who was, with his mouth, very persuasive indeed.

"Mmm," Dr. Roger Janek said. "You taste like heaven."

His touch thrilled her in a way that made Judy's throat tighten with need. All that trapped energy of his was about to be exerted in gratifying the two of them.

"Please, Roger."

"Soon," he whispered.

She stroked him, hoping to build his need to her level, so that he would be unable to wait a moment longer.

He laughed—a deep, rich sound that raced the length of her. "Yes, I want you, and I can hardly stand it," he admitted. "But there's something I want from you first."

"What?" she asked, barely able to speak.

"You'll know," he told her, and set about fulfilling his promise.

Judy had sworn never to trust a doctor's love again. But now her own body was betraying her. . . .

SIGNET

ONYX

The Best Medicine

Elizabeth Neff Walker

A SIGNET BOOK

SIGNET
Published by the Penguin Group
Penguin Books USA Inc., 375 Hudson Street,
New York, New York 10014, U.S.A.
Penguin Books Ltd, 27 Wrights Lane,
London W8 5TZ, England
Penguin Books Australia Ltd, Ringwood,
Victoria, Australia
Penguin Books Canada Ltd, 10 Alcorn Avenue,
Toronto, Ontario, Canada M4V 3B2
Penguin Books (N.Z.) Ltd, 182–190 Wairau Road,
Auckland 10, New Zealand

Penguin Books Ltd, Registered Offices:
Harmondsworth, Middlesex, England

First published by Signet, an imprint of Dutton Signet,
a division of Penguin Books USA Inc.

First Printing, February, 1996
10 9 8 7 6 5 4 3 2 1

Printed in the United States of America

PUBLISHER'S NOTE
This is a work of fiction. Names, characters, places, and incidents either are the product of the author's imagination or are used fictitiously, and any resemblance to actual persons, living or dead, events, or locales is entirely coincidental.

With special thanks to Miranda Coffey
for her valuable insight and her valued friendship

Chapter One

Roger Janek had been back in his own house in San Francisco for more than a month when he had the accident. It was not so much that he had been careless as that he had simply misjudged distances on the shadowy street. No one was injured. Roger, his concentration distracted by a cat racing across the street, had simply misjudged the distance between his own car, another car going the other way, and the dark debris box he was passing on his right.

His car, a four-year-old Audi, incurred a surprising amount of damage for such a minor accident. What was worse, the annoying vehicle would not run. The fender was mashed right up against the right front tire and refused to budge even when he wielded a crowbar against it.

Unlike most of the other doctors he knew, Roger

did not have a car phone, which necessitated his hiking two blocks to Geary Boulevard to find a pay phone. He was almost near enough to the hospital to walk there, but the journey seemed pointless since what he needed was the Automobile Association in any case. And he was going to miss the monthly meeting of his grief support group.

Roger tugged carelessly at the lobe of one ear as he dug in his pocket with the other hand for some dimes. He surveyed the handful of coins he withdrew and chose two, before noticing that the phone in front of which he stood was obviously out of order. The receiver rested in its holder, but the cord swung uselessly free from its connection. In frustration Roger swatted the metal frame.

A horn honked behind him, and he wondered briefly if one of the citizenry objected to this mild gesture of annoyance. As he turned to see, a dark-haired woman leaned out of the window of a car and called, "Do you have a problem, Dr. Janek?"

She looked familiar, in a way that made him feel a little sad. Probably from the hospital, then. He stepped closer and recognized her as a nurse from the oncology floor, one of the nurses who had taken care of his wife, Kerri. "The damn phone's busted," he said. "I've had an accident, and I need to call AAA."

"You okay?" she asked, peering up and down at

him as though she might notice a broken arm or battered flesh.

"Yeah, I'm fine. My car's not." He was dredging his mind for a name. As an anesthesiologist, he didn't have many dealings with the floor nurses, but this one he should know. She'd helped arrange for the wedding in Kerri's hospital room almost a year ago. Maybe was even the one who'd brought Kerri the garland of flowers for her hair.

"It's Judy Povalski," she said, relieving him. "Sixth floor East. Let me drive you to a working phone."

"That would be great." Roger climbed into her car, an older Honda Civic, and closed the door twice before it caught. "There's bound to be one pretty close."

"For sure there's one two blocks down, though I suppose it could be broken, too. We'll check."

Without further comment, she drew away from the curb and raced through the next intersection. Roger recognized her driving style as faintly similar to his own and regarded her with curiosity. "Do people complain about your driving?" he asked.

"Frequently." She glanced over at him and laughed. "Not usually within the first block, though."

"I just wondered. They complain about mine all the time. Even Kerri did."

"You can only expect so much tolerance, even from someone who loves you."

The things people said didn't usually bother him

so much anymore. But she said it almost as though Kerri might be waiting at home for him, and he felt the dreaded ache in his chest. "I suppose not," he murmured.

"She was a very special woman," Judy continued. "Truly remarkable in her acceptance of her illness and in trying to help everyone around her accept it, too."

"Thank you." It was the only thing he could think of to say. Most people hesitated to talk to him about Kerri, and he often wished they would. Certainly no one ignored him. In fact, everyone had been amazingly kind. But life continued, and even his best friends assumed he was continuing with it, in a way he hadn't really achieved yet. Angel Crawford, who had helped him all along, was busy finishing the last month of her residency and was pregnant as could be. He didn't see as much of her and Cliff as he used to. Nan had moved to Belvedere with Steve. Jerry pretty much lived at Rachel's. Everything outside him was constantly changing.

"Check if this one's working," Judy said, breaking into his thoughts. "Then I'll drive you back to your car."

They were stopped in front of a phone booth. "You probably have something better to do."

"Nothing that won't keep."

At first it had embarrassed him to have people do things for him, perfect strangers and bare acquaintances, but Jerry had convinced him that people felt better for helping, and Jerry was a psychiatrist, so he should know. Roger climbed agilely out of the car and checked out the phone, which gave a dial tone when he lifted it. But he had to look up the AAA number in the phone book and before he'd riffled many pages, Judy yelled a number from the car.

"I know it by heart," she explained. "I have to call them all the time."

When he had explained his dilemma to the person who answered, he was informed that a truck would be there in half an hour to forty-five minutes. Roger sighed and returned to Judy's car. "I'm just a few blocks away. Over on Lake Street near Twenty-fifth."

"Right." Judy whipped the little car around the block like a race car driver. When she stopped in front of his car, her headlights illuminating the mangled right front, she whistled. "They'll total it," she said with conviction.

"What do you mean, total it? Who will?"

"The insurance company, of course. If it costs more to repair than the *Blue Book,* they total it."

"Well, I don't want it totaled. It has sentimental value."

"Was it Kerri's car?" she asked, surprised.

"No, but we drove everywhere together in it. It won't be that expensive to repair."

"Ha! You probably haven't had bodywork done on

a car lately," she said knowledgeably. "It costs a fortune."

Roger wasn't going to argue with her. No matter what it cost, he was going to have the car repaired. "Well, thanks for driving me over, Judy. I'll wait in my car."

"No problem." She watched as he climbed out, and then she rolled down her window as he walked across in front of her car. "When you were a teenager, did you get into trouble?"

"Me?" Surprised, he turned back to her. "Nothing important. Why do you ask?"

She shrugged. "I just wondered if all teenage boys do. Sometimes that's the impression people give you."

"Do you have a teenage boy?" Roger tried to remember whether he knew if she was married. He drew a total blank. In the dark he couldn't see if she wore a ring.

"No, but I live with my sister and hers. Your car reminded me. Larry took her car last week without asking and managed to do that kind of damage to it." She made a gesture indicating her dismissal of the subject. "Sorry. I didn't mean to insinuate that you'd have been some kind of troubled kid when you were younger."

But Roger's attention had been captured by a subject very close to his experience. He walked back to the driver's side window. "I didn't get into trouble like that, but my brother Carl did. Not that I was an angel, mind you. But I was always kind of too interested in science, and pretty much a loner."

"Larry isn't a loner," Judy said tartly. "In fact, he seems to be very easily led astray. Or, maybe, he does the leading."

"No father in the household, I gather."

She shook her head. "His father was killed in a car accident over a year ago."

"Well, my brother got into trouble even with my father in the house, and my father's a great guy. Sometimes I think that's what Carl was rebelling against." Roger sighed. "He didn't get over it for a long time, until my uncle stepped in to help."

"I'm hoping Larry will grow out of it one of these days. Well, thanks, Dr. Janek. Good luck with the car."

"It's Roger. And good luck with your nephew."

If he hadn't had to wait half an hour alone in his car after she left, he would probably never have come up with the idea. Say the tow truck had showed up immediately after her taillights had disappeared down the street. He would have been so involved in the details of the car being attached to the towing bar and deciding where to have it towed, that Judy's remarks would have instantly dissolved from his mind.

Later, in the OR dressing room, Angel's husband, Cliff, had tried to discourage him. "You can't get involved in someone else's life that way," he insisted as they changed clothes after a colon resection. Cliff, a big bear of a man with unruly black hair and a slightly overbearing manner, said, "Face it, Roger. You're vulnerable right now. You're looking for something to distract you and make you feel useful again. You can't just choose to take on someone's troubled teenager. You don't even know him."

"True," Roger agreed. Since the death of his wife, his youthful face had aged, but the difference was only noticeable to his friends. He was of medium height, with a curly brown mass of hair, a wiry build, and an excess of nervous habits like tugging on the drawstring of his scrub pants, which he was currently doing. "But people become Big Brothers to kids all the time, and they're kids they don't even know. At least this kid belongs to someone's sister. To me that makes more sense than choosing someone anonymous."

"Neither makes any sense to me," Cliff assured him as he tossed his scrub suit in a laundry bin. "What do you know about helping disturbed teenagers? Zilch. You don't even have any kids of your own."

"No, but I *was* a kid once upon a time. Like you and everybody else. I bet Angel wouldn't think it was such a stupid idea."

"Angel gets misty-eyed at the sound of a baby crying these days," Cliff confessed without rancor. "She can already picture us in the wilds of Wisconsin sitting on a screened porch with the new arrival in a cradle her mother saved from thirty years ago."

"I'm going to miss you two, even though I don't see that much of you these days."

Cliff's bristling eyebrows rose a fraction. "Is this a subtle hint that we should have you over to dinner?"

"Of course not! I know how busy you are." Roger rubbed his temple absently. "Hell, Cliff, this would give me something to do. Something important."

"Are you back on the 'Rescue the Teenager' kick? Roger, anesthesiology is important. You protect people's lives during surgery. You train the next generation of doctors to have iron nerves and impressive skills. Take some kind of advanced training, do some research, travel to a conference, write a paper. There are a dozen things you could do that wouldn't involve getting entangled in someone else's problems."

But Roger wasn't paying much attention. Truth be told, he'd already decided. Of course, Judy and her sister might not be interested in his trying to help out, and if they weren't he'd have to find some other project. But this was, at least temporarily, a project that he felt almost compelled to attempt. There were several reasons. His brother Carl was one, certainly. What if someone hadn't stepped in and turned Carl around?

But another reason was Kerri. She'd been a teacher, and Roger had heard her numerous times discuss how important it was for a child to have someone in their lives who proved the right kind of model. She had said that, as well-intentioned as they were, a child's parents weren't always the right people.

When he'd described his brother Carl to her, Kerri had nodded and said, "Yes, that's what I mean. Your parents are obviously good people, but they lived on a different plane than Carl. They were intellectuals and sophisticated in a way that made him seem to them like a changeling. You have a restless kind of energy, too, Roger, but you channeled it in ways they could understand. Carl obviously didn't."

She had said something then that he grasped at now: "If you'd been grown then, I think you would have understood Carl, even though you were so different. But you were only a kid, too." She had also said how much she regretted that they wouldn't have children of their own. Roger hadn't thought of it that much then, but he'd thought a lot about it since her death, that he would never be a father. God, she would have been the perfect mother—patient and loving and generous and understanding.

Kerri would have approved of his trying to help a troubled teenager. Roger was sure of it.

Judy Povalski worked on the oncology floor at Fielding Medical Center. She had switched there two years before, after working at SF General and

Fielding over the previous ten years as a circulating nurse and a scrub nurse in the operating room. Though people thought it a strange move, from an atmosphere of high tension and excitement to one of frequent desperation and gloom, Judy found the work on the cancer unit more rewarding. Instead of anesthetized patients, here were people in the very throes of the most difficult period of their lives—living with disease, dying of disease. She could be of far more assistance here than handing over instruments in a sterile if companionable environment.

After a year on the floor, she'd been offered the assistant head nurse position, but she had refused it. Administrative work was of little interest to her. Again people shook their heads wonderingly. Had she no ambition at all? Didn't she want to get somewhere in her field? No, she told them, she wanted to do precisely what she was doing. Very codependent, her friends said. Judy couldn't be bothered with glib labels. She liked working with people, liked being the one who brought comfort into their shattered lives. That's what nurses, much more than doctors, were able to do.

Judy didn't think much of it when she saw Roger Janek come onto the floor. Some of the patients on Six East were there for surgery, and Roger would come to talk with them the previous day to get a history. He didn't need to have much interaction with the nurses, however, so when he headed straight for the nurses' station, she raised her brows inquiringly at him.

"What's up, Dr. Janek?" she asked. "Everything okay with your car?"

He shrugged. "The insurance company totaled it, just like you said they would. And it did sound outrageously expensive to have it repaired right, so I just had them fix it enough to make it run for now. Cliff's trying to talk me into a new Saab convertible. He says they're really sharp."

"They are. Halverson has one, bright red. You could ask him how he likes it."

"Oh, God, I could have the same car as Halverson," he muttered. "Lucky me."

Judy knew better than to ask him if he had something against the heart surgeon. Halverson's reputation in the operating room was legend. He was possibly the only surgeon at Fielding who treated the anesthesiologists like water boys. "Well, it might not suit your style right now, anyhow. They're a bit sporty."

"I don't know that my style was ever sporty, and it certainly doesn't feel like that now. I think Cliff was sublimating his own wish. Angel's apparently suggested a station wagon."

"Horrors!" Judy said with a laugh. "That's what having kids will do to you, I guess."

"Speaking of which . . ." Roger surveyed the congested area and waved toward the conference room down the hall. "Do you have a minute for me to talk with you?"

Mystified, Judy nodded and followed him down the corridor. He was wearing scrubs and a patterned scrub cap. His wiry build was almost indiscernible in the folds of the blue scrubs, but he carried himself with a barely controlled energy that was recognizable even from a distance. No one who knew him was unaware of his nervous habits, which were generally accepted as evidence of his restrained energy. Judy found them touching.

The conference room was empty, and he switched on the light and left the door open, taking a seat at the small rectangular table and waving her to another one. "This is going to sound crazy, I guess." He tugged at the lobe of his right ear. "The other night you mentioned that your nephew had been getting in trouble."

"My nephew? Well, yes, but nothing really bad."

"So far," he said bluntly. "Things usually go from bad to worse."

"God, I hope not. But I don't understand what you're getting at."

"I've been thinking about him—your nephew."

Judy frowned. "I didn't mean to bother you about Larry, Dr. Janek. The question just sort of popped out of me."

"Roger," he reminded her. "And I'm glad it did." He knocked his scrub cap off with an impatient hand, revealing hair that was only slightly more curly than her own. His was a rich brown, though, and hers a gleaming black that made people question her about Irish origins.

Judy waited a little impatiently for him to continue, thinking that he was going to offer some advice. Which was thoughtful of him, perhaps, but a bit presumptuous. For some reason, even unmarried men seemed to think they knew a great deal about raising boys.

"Maybe I could help him," Roger finally blurted.

"Help him?" Judy cocked her head inquiringly. "I can't imagine how, Doc—Roger. He's a teenager."

"Well, exactly. That's when boys tend to get into trouble, and they can keep on going bad if someone doesn't step in and take hold of them."

Confused, Judy protested, "But you've never even seen him. You don't have any relationship with him. I don't understand what you're saying."

Roger took a deep breath and exhaled quickly. "I'm not being very clear. I'm restless, Judy. I need to do something useful, really useful. Not anesthesia. That's my work. I need to do something that will make a difference. Maybe I could step into his life—what did you say his name was, Larry?—and help turn him around."

"But you have no experience with boys," she pointed out. "What could you possibly do that would help? He already has a tutor for math and belongs to a sports club that Liza can scarcely afford, all so he'll have male authority figures in his life. He's got teachers and coaches and neighbors, and you aren't any of those things. I beg your pardon for being so frank, Dr. Janek, but it seems to me your good intentions probably exceed your experience."

"They do," he agreed with a grimace. "It was stupid of me to think I could help."

"I didn't say that! You're being incredibly generous to make that kind of offer. I understand that you'd *like* to help." Judy was starting to feel guilty. How could she just shoot down someone with such good intentions, someone whose wife had died within the year? But his offer came completely out of left field, with no tie to any personal relationship. The whole thing made her uncomfortable.

Judy rose briskly and pushed her chair back under the table. "Look, I really ought to get back to my work. They'll wonder where I've gotten to. But I want to thank you for the thought. Really, it was . . . um . . . very thoughtful of you, Dr. Janek." She started backing toward the door. "I'll bet there are lots of things you could do that would be, you know, just the right thing for someone. That would make a difference." With a small wave of her hand, she fled the room.

Well, I really screwed that up, Roger decided as he retrieved his scrub cap from the table. What the hell was I thinking of? I don't know these people, and they don't know me. Plus, I'm not some kind of authority on wayward teenagers. I just wanted the boy to know that someone else cared about him. But how do I know if I'd care about him? Probably he's a little jerk who'd drive me crazy if I ever met him and had any responsibility for his actions.

That woman must think I've completely lost it, he thought, and considered tracking Judy down again to prove that he hadn't. Something—probably Cliff's voice in his head—warned him that that wouldn't be a smart idea, and he abandoned it. After checking his watch and finding that he wasn't due down in surgery for half an hour, he wandered through the medical center until he came upon Jerry's office, thinking to have a little chat with his psychiatrist friend. But there was no one in the office, and the first nurse he ran into explained that Dr. Stoner was away at a conference for a few days. Roger sighed and headed for surgery.

Chapter Two

Though it might have made an entertaining story, Judy didn't mention Roger Janek's strange suggestion to anyone at the hospital. She did wonder if it didn't show that he was still a bit unsteady from his grief at Kerri's death. Not in a way that would affect his work, but perhaps in a way that indicated he could use a little emotional support.

Her favorite of the psychiatrists at Fielding, Jerry Stoner, turned out to be away for a few days, and there was no one else with whom she felt comfortable discussing something that might be used to damage Dr. Janek's reputation in careless hands. But she was disconcerted enough by the incident that she took it home to her sister to sort out in her own mind.

After dinner, when Larry should have been helping, Judy and Liza found themselves putting away leftovers, washing dishes, and scrubbing pots. Having exhausted their store of potential remedies, they shied away from discussing their failed attempts to force Larry to take on his share of the household tasks. Both women knew the boy was out of their control. Liza, as his mother, had tried, though not always consistently, the whole gamut of parental tricks—pleading, threatening, grounding, not preparing meals—to no avail.

The sixteen-year-old Larry seemed to inhabit a world of his own, sometimes closing himself into his room, sometimes vanishing for hours. He wasn't so much rude or oppositional to those around him, as he was seemingly heedless of their expectations of him, no matter how often they were clearly expressed. The school authorities were adamant that his behavior of cutting classes, not turning in homework, paying scant attention to school rules, had to be changed, but they offered few useful suggestions. The sports club people had initially been hopeful that they could interest the boy in some activity, but they had become discouraged when he seldom attended their program.

Larry didn't seem to care much about anything, except driving. Liza had thought that would prove a way to control him, but he had taken her car keys and driven without her permission, managing to damage her car in the process. He had been grounded for a month and expressed regret for the incident, but neither woman could believe that he realized the gravity of the situation.

It had been Judy's night to cook, and she'd made a spicy spaghetti sauce that Larry had enthusiastically complimented. He was not, she reminded herself, without redeeming virtues. In fact, she loved him dearly and was more distressed than angered by his behavior. When he had drifted off and she was putting away the salad dressing and stacking the salad bowls on the counter, she related Roger Janek's offer to her sister.

Liza regarded her curiously. "How did he know about Larry? Had you said something?"

"Only when I drove him to make a call to AAA." Judy narrowed her blue eyes, trying to remember precisely what she *had* said. "I think I asked him if he'd ever gotten into trouble as a teenager. You know, one of those things that just pop out of your mouth."

"Out of *your* mouth," Liza said, but not unkindly. "I don't think it would occur to me to ask a doctor if he'd gotten in trouble as a teenager. Doctors intimidate me at the best of times."

"They're just human, like the rest of us," Judy said, not for the first time, though she was never sure she meant it. Doctors didn't intimidate her, but they frequently disappointed her expectations of their humanity in attending their patients. "You have to understand this guy married a woman last summer who was dying. That may have been when you and Larry were back at Mom's."

Liza's eyes widened. "How awful. But if she was dying, why did he marry her?"

"He loved her. And I could kind of see his point. If she'd died and she'd just been his girlfriend, people wouldn't have understood her importance in his life. He wanted everyone to know that, and he wanted *her* to know it."

"And she died?"

"Oh, yes. Within a few weeks. She'd been my patient, so I was involved in the arrangements for the wedding and all."

"So," Liza mused as she scoured a cast-iron skillet, "you think Dr. Janek is still shaken by this woman's death, and that has something to do with his offering to help out with Larry?"

"Well, he's had a difficult year. He even had to move out of his house because of insomnia. He shared a flat with a neurology fellow, Nan LeBaron, for a while. Now I gather he's back home, so maybe he's looking for a way to distract himself."

"He probably doesn't know what today's teenagers are like." Liza dried her hands on a terry-cloth dish towel, which she then tossed over a ceramic cow's head on the wall. "Still, I wish *someone* would come along who could take Larry in hand."

Judy was incredulous. "You don't mean you wish I hadn't turned him down, do you?"

"Of course you had to turn him down. I'm just so exhausted with the effort, Judy. And I'm not doing him any good. I'm afraid he's going to get into more serious trouble if something doesn't happen soon to turn him around. And I'll be responsible."

"You've done everything you could."

Liza shrugged. "It hasn't been enough. I've been totally ineffective. If only Bob hadn't died. He was so good with Larry. Remember how they used to play basketball in the driveway? I could watch from the kitchen window while I got dinner. And Larry had just made the basketball team before Bob died. Bob was so proud of him!"

"I remember." Judy gave her sister's shoulders a fierce hug. "I wish we could have gotten Larry to try out for basketball at his school here. It would have been so good for him to have something to do."

"He said kids in San Francisco were much better than the boys on a small-town team. He insisted that he wouldn't be good enough. Do you think that's true?"

"I don't know. Maybe. But he could play basketball at the sports center, and he doesn't." Judy stared down into the fenced backyard below, a frustrated frown wrinkling her brow. "Do you think that psychologist you took him to might have been wrong? That maybe he's still really depressed by Bob's death?"

"Dr. Bloom seemed very certain it was more than

grief, that Larry was having trouble adjusting to the move and growing up and . . . well, a lot of things."

Judy said caustically, "Doctors aren't always right. But it's a shame Larry wasn't willing to see him for a while."

"No matter what it is, Judy, what can I do? I brought him here because it seemed a good idea to get us both away from all the things that reminded us of Bob in the valley. This was like a fresh start."

"I know. But he's an adolescent, and that's a tough time for kids even when they aren't uprooted and haven't lost their fathers. I just wish we could reach him somehow."

"I've tried everything I know of, Judy. I'm near the end of my rope."

"You haven't given up on Larry, have you?"

Liza stood with slumped shoulders, her pixie face drawn. "Of course not, but something has to change, Judy. This can't go on. Every time the phone rings, I'm afraid it will be trouble." Her eyes filled with tears. "What happened to him, Judy? He was such an adorable kid."

Though Judy had lived in San Francisco most of Larry's life, she knew this was true from her frequent visits to her hometown. Liza, who had gotten pregnant when she was seventeen, had been madly in love with her Bob. Their families had doubted the wisdom of their marrying so young, but had consented under the circumstances.

Still children themselves, Liza and Bob had not fully understood the responsibilities that would fall on them as parents, but they had done their best. Bob had worked in a hardware store, and Liza had learned word processing. Their child *had* been adorable, and thoroughly lovable, but a handful even then.

Judy remembered her mother's worried warning that Larry would need a strong father to keep him in line. But Bob had been killed in a traffic accident caused by an unexpected tule fog, leaving a grief-stricken widow and a confused, rebellious son. Judy had welcomed Liza's decision to move to San Francisco, thinking she could be of help to these two unhappy people.

"We'll spend more time with him," Judy heard herself say. "We'll take him on a special vacation. We'll do *something*."

"But what?" Liza asked wearily. "School's out next week, and Larry will have the whole summer to get in trouble. He's too old to put in day camp. He says there are no jobs. Mom offered to take him, but frankly, Judy, I wouldn't do that to her."

Judy cringed at the thought. "No, I don't think that would be wise. How about summer school?"

Liza shook her head. "You know he wouldn't go, especially since he hasn't failed anything." She moved disconsolately to stand beside her sister at the kitchen window. "Do you think maybe that doctor could actually do something with him?"

Judy snorted. "Liza, he must be my age, and he's never had kids. What could he possibly know? And he's not in any shape to be trying to help someone else. *He's* the one who needs help."

"I suppose." The evening light made Liza's face look pale. Her light brown hair appeared drained of its usual reddish highlights and as lusterless as she did herself at the moment. "Of course, there's a chance I'll lose my job, and I could be at home with Larry until I found another one."

"Is there some danger of losing your job?"

Liza's sigh was almost inaudible. "They're cutting back. Jennifer was let go last week. Everyone is afraid there are more cuts in store, and I'm one of the most recent word processors hired. Law firms don't need as many of us with their workload down."

"Well, you'd get unemployment for a while. And you have the insurance money set aside."

"That's for Larry's education."

"And emergencies. Why haven't you said something before about work?"

It was hard to tell in the twilight, but Judy thought a flush came to her sister's cheeks. "Well, there's a guy there who really likes my work. I think he'd make an effort to save my job if they considered laying me off."

"I see," Judy said, but she wasn't sure that she did.

Larry appeared in the kitchen doorway, shrugging into a jean jacket. He was a tall boy, with sad brown eyes and shaggy brown hair. "I'm going over to Michael's. I won't be late."

"Do you have homework?" his mother asked automatically.

"Nah. Nothing important."

"You don't want to take a chance of failing something this late in the year," she pointed out.

"I'm not going to, Mom."

Judy saw Liza's fingers automatically dig in her pants pockets, where she now kept her car keys. As Larry disappeared down the hall, Judy just as automatically reached for her purse, where she kept a second set of keys to her sister's car. "They're here," she said.

"See what we do?" Liza raked short fingers through her hair. "See how far it's gotten? We don't trust him. We can't. Is that going to go on forever? I don't think I could bear that, Judy. We have to find a way to turn this around."

Which was the first time that Judy, reluctantly, considered Roger Janek's offer. Maybe Roger could give the boy something that his mother and his aunt could not. Probably Larry needed a solid male role model in his life. And, oddly, it might be just what Roger needed to set his own life on a more even keel.

* * *

Roger stood in his garage regarding the damaged Audi with frustration. He had had it made drivable after he'd heard the insurance company's pronouncement. Whether he would decide to use the insurance money to have it properly repaired, or to get a new car, he hadn't decided. Though he preferred the former course, he knew the latter was much smarter. His sentimental attachment to the Audi was out of proportion to the role it had played in his life with Kerri. In fact, he had intended to get a new car for the two of them, had some miracle happened and she'd lived longer.

The garage door remained open as he sorted through the contents of the glove compartment. He glanced up at a honking from the end of his short driveway and smiled at the woman who waved at him from her Rabbit. Angel had been his mainstay during the hard days after Kerri's death, and she had remained closely in touch with him right up to the present. But her advanced pregnancy, and this being the last month of her family-practice residency at Fielding, were cutting into her available time. To say nothing of her marriage to Cliff. Roger left his task to sprint down the drive to her car.

"God, you look glowing," he said as he opened the driver side door for her. "I always thought that was a myth about pregnancy. Something to sort of fool men into believing their wives hadn't swallowed balloons.

Are you still resisting the urge to find out the baby's sex?"

Angel climbed cautiously out of her car. "Yes, though the last ultrasound was fairly obvious, and very appropriate, when you think about it."

"It's a boy." Roger grinned. "I hope that's okay with you."

She tucked her arm through his as they walked sedately up the drive. "Of course. I'm just hoping we'll have a chance to get settled in Wisconsin before he's born." She glanced at the open garage. "Cliff told me about your car. I'm sorry. Going to get a new one?"

"Probably." He opened the red front door of the shingled house and waited while she made her way to the comfortable armchair in the living room. It was "her" chair when she was there, because she could put her feet up on the hassock and sink back into its soft contours. "Would you like a glass of wine?"

"Better make it a mineral water, or a soda. I can only stay a few minutes, but I wanted to see how you were doing."

When Roger returned with two sodas, the only drinks he could find in the refrigerator, he took a seat on the sofa opposite her. "It's kind of nice being back here. I'm not having any trouble sleeping or anything. I've already got the garden in shape, and I'm looking for the next project."

Angel pushed back a strand of auburn hair. Even

with his assurances, her gray-green eyes regarded him with concern. "I've been hearing something about your wanting to get involved with a troubled teenager."

"Yeah, Cliff thought I was nuts, and frankly so did Judy when I suggested it. I guess I embarrassed her, bringing it up." He twisted the flexible band of his watch in a hazardous fashion before continuing. "But I thought I'd talk to Jerry when he gets back. Maybe he'll know someone I could help that way."

"You're certain you want to work with teenage boys? You'd never mentioned it before."

"It occurred to me when Judy mentioned her nephew getting into trouble. I have a brother who was a real problem as a teenager, but an uncle took him under his wing. I thought I could try to do something like that, something really worth doing."

Angel shifted in the overstuffed chair and leaned toward him. "It wasn't only Cliff who talked with me about it, Roger. Knowing we're good friends, Judy came to me today, asking what I thought about your suggestion. Apparently her sister's about at the end of her rope with the boy. Judy would like to help, but she doesn't know what to do that they haven't already tried. She was worried that your offer might mean you were a little unstable because of your grief. That upset her, for your sake. But she also wondered whether I thought maybe you *could* help in some way. Because they're kind of desperate."

Roger allowed the wristband to snap back with a smack. "Really? She'd consider it? Let me get involved with the kid?"

"Well, let's say her sister is desperate enough to consider it. Judy still thinks it's a little strange."

"I suppose it is. I wish Jerry had been around for me to ask. Rachel says he'll be back on Sunday. Should I talk to Judy?"

"Let's you and me talk first." Angel swirled the ice in her soda. "It's been my impression that you were getting better, Roger. That you were accepting Kerri's death more thoroughly, and that you were moving on with your life. I mean, you've moved back to your house. Nan felt a little guilty about that, you know. She was afraid her not being around much might have forced that on you before you were ready."

"Steve invited me to move in with them in Belvedere. I'm not sure he was kidding."

Angel laughed. "Steve's sense of humor takes some getting used to. But since Nan kept the flat near the hospital, and you could have stayed there if you'd needed to, I assumed you moved back here because you were ready."

"I was. I am. I still miss Kerri like mad, but that awful emptiness has settled down somewhat. I'm not looking to work with the boy just because I want to fill up an empty place. It's more because I have some energy back, and a need to do something useful. You know, Angel, it was terrible not being able to do anything for Kerri. It made me realize that being a doctor isn't as important as we're all led to believe." He waved a dismissive hand. "Not that I mean to discourage you in any way."

"Every day I see the limits of our abilities as doctors. I know what you mean. I wouldn't choose any other profession, but it's made me realize there's more, and less, to this job than healing. But family practice has more scope that way than anesthesiology. You don't have much ongoing patient contact. Maybe rather than involve yourself in someone's life, which could be messy, you need to find a place in your field where you'd feel more connected—intensive care or pain management or something like that."

Roger appeared thoughtful for a few minutes. Thinking for him was a physical as well as mental process. His fingers drummed on the arm of the sofa, his foot tapped insistently against the hardwood floor. After a while he straightened in his seat.

"You may be right. I went into the field because I felt awkward with patients, you know? Now I feel really comfortable doing what I do, but I don't have much of a relationship with the people I treat. I've learned how to make them feel confidence in me, and I've certainly become very skillful at anesthetizing patients. But I'm only important in someone's life for a day. That's pretty puny. I'm not saying it isn't important work in the overall picture of things. But maybe I do need to do something more important, right now.

"You see," he said, looking down at his knees, "I'm alive. Kerri's dead and I'm alive, and somehow I should deserve to be alive by doing something really worthwhile. Does that make any sense to you?"

"Well, the rest of us don't have to come up with a reason to be alive, Roger, so it tells me you're still suffering the effects of Kerri's death, but probably not in a terribly unhealthy way. I wish Jerry were around for you to talk to. Do people in your grief support group feel that way sometimes?"

"The younger ones, I guess. Nobody seems to know what to do about it."

Angel rubbed her thumb thoughtfully along the sweating glass, not saying anything for some time. Roger slumped back on the sofa, looking morose. He wanted Angel to approve of his plan about the boy because he respected her judgment. Cliff wouldn't really consider such a project, but Angel would understand the reasons behind it, and be able to project an outcome.

After a while she sighed and said, "Roger, I want you to think about what could happen here. With the best intentions in the world, you could really end up making yourself and this kid miserable. What if he rejects you? What if he doesn't like you? Teenagers are a breed apart. There never seems any rhyme or reason for what they do, how they feel about things. And what if you ended up hating him? They can be little idiots. How much tolerance do you have, especially for a kid who isn't even related to you?

"And then there's the matter of Judy and her sister. They could start to put a great deal of hope in the possibility of your accomplishing something with the boy. They could be very disappointed if you failed. *You* could be disappointed if you failed. There's something particularly upsetting about investing time and energy and emotion into something like this and having it blow up in your face. Are you in any emotional condition to handle that?"

It wasn't that Roger hadn't skimmed over all these possibilities in his mind. It was just that having another person point them out to him was rather sobering. Any of them, all of them, could happen. "I understand what you're saying. And I know you're only thinking of what's best for everyone, but it sounds like this kid needs someone. His dad died only a year or so ago. It's a risk, actually, for all of us. I don't know if it would be fair of me to ask Judy and her sister and the boy to take that risk, but I'm certainly willing to take it for myself."

"How are you going to learn what to do for him?"

"I'll read. I'll talk with Jerry. I'll ask friends who have teenagers. But mostly, Angel, I'll have to work from my own instincts, and from my experience with my brother. Maybe I can help this kid. I think it's worth a try. Don't you?"

"Actually," Angel said with a smile, "I do. I'd certainly talk with Jerry and be guided by him, but if it's any help to you, Roger, I'm with you."

He expelled the deep breath he'd unconsciously been holding. "Thanks, Angel. I needed that."

Chapter Three

Judy felt somewhat reassured after her talk with Angel Crawford. Angel was a levelheaded woman, and Judy felt she could trust Angel's judgment that Roger was not suffering from some exacerbated grief crisis. Nonetheless, Judy made no move to speak with Roger, waiting instead to see if he would approach her again. Several days passed before he showed up on Six East.

Toward the end of a Tuesday afternoon, he came trotting down the corridor, his scrubs partially covered with a doctor's white coat. He looked eager and animated, and though he spotted her quickly and smiled, he stopped in his progress to answer another nurse's question before popping up at Judy's side at the nurses' station.

"Have you got a minute?" he asked hopefully.

"Sure." She beckoned him into the chart room and

leaned against the wall. "Dr. Crawford probably told you I asked about you and this idea of your getting involved with my nephew."

"Yeah. She and I talked about it. I was glad you'd given the idea some thought, Judy. I was afraid you'd dismissed it."

Judy grimaced. "I had, but my sister made me reconsider. So you're still interested?"

"Absolutely. Angel wanted me to talk to Jerry Stoner first, and he's been away."

"What did Dr. Stoner say?"

"He told me I was a glutton for punishment, but not to a psychotic level. Or maybe it was neurotic. I always forget which he says, because he makes it sound so ordinary. Do all psychiatrists do that?"

"No, not the ones I've known." Judy considered him for a moment. The face that had seemed so boyish a year ago had aged, though not in a haggard way. If she hadn't known him before, she would probably simply take it for the mature face of a thirty-five-year-old man who had responsibilities. His boundless energy still leaked out in the drumming of his fingertips on the chart rack. "Why don't you come over and meet my sister? The two of you could talk about how to help Larry."

"Wouldn't you be there?"

"Well, sure, if you wanted me to be, or Liza did. I don't know that I'm just full of suggestions. Everything I've tried has been a disaster."

"Like what?"

"Oh, I took him to a ball game a few weeks ago. I mean, what could go wrong at a ball game, right?"

"What did go wrong?"

Judy sighed. "Larry got bored when the Giants were losing so badly and threw popcorn at people in the rows ahead of us. It was pretty awful when the usher came down and told us we'd have to leave."

Roger whistled. "So we won't try baseball right away. Are there any other sports or courses he likes?"

"He used to play basketball, but he won't do it in San Francisco. He liked skateboarding until he learned to drive. Now he kind of ignores it. He's bright enough, but he doesn't have any interest in school classes, so he gets in trouble there." She asked with a rueful smile, "Have I discouraged you?"

"Not yet." Roger pulled at his right earlobe. "So when can I meet your sister, Judy? How about if I take both of you out to dinner somewhere quiet, and we can talk?"

"I suppose that would be all right. When?"

"Tonight?"

Judy laughed. "No, not tonight. I have a class, and Liza put something in the Crock-Pot this morning for dinner. Tomorrow might be okay, but I'd have to check with her."

Roger pulled a pad of Post-It notes toward him and scribbled his phone number. "Tomorrow's great.

Give me a call later, would you, to let me know? What kind of class?"

"Computer. I'm trying to improve my feeble skills and work myself into the twentieth century."

"Hmm. Do you have one at home?"

"No, but they give us extra time at the school so you can practice. Liza can answer some of my questions."

Roger nodded and scratched his head. "I'll talk with you later."

Judy watched him bound off down the corridor. He was a very fine person, good-hearted and honorable. And there was a renewed vigor about him that showed even in the way he walked, an animation in his face that had been damped down for too long. Maybe Larry was just the challenge Roger needed to pull him the rest of the way out of the doldrums. Certainly, Liza was ready to grasp any outside help that offered even a glimmer of hope. And Judy realized that she herself felt a burgeoning confidence that Roger, just because he was a solid, energetic, and enthusiastic person, would be a really good influence on her nephew.

With a sigh Judy bent to the task she'd been working on before Roger's arrival. Writing up patient-care plans was tedious and kept her from the rewarding part of her job, patient contact. Formulating the plans was one of the many ways in which floor nursing differed from operating-room nursing. The operating room had been dramatic, and Judy had loved that atmosphere. In the operating room there had been a special sense of teamwork, of camaraderie. On the floor there was often a palpable tension among the nurses, and between doctors and nurses.

When Judy had worked in the OR, she had been proud of keeping a level head and of being creatively organized. During operations for which she'd been scrub nurse many times, she could anticipate what instrument the surgeon would call for next and have it ready to slap in his hand before he even asked for it. Sometimes that coordination made operations feel like dancing a ballet.

Though she knew she was regarded as a handmaiden in the OR, she'd considered herself a very good handmaiden, perhaps even a remarkable handmaiden. It was not until she overheard a surgeon saying to a colleague, "You know, the one with the curly hair—what's-her-name," that she realized she was, in many of their minds, interchangeable with every other efficient operating-room nurse.

Still, it had taken a long time for Judy to realize that the excitement of the OR masked a very real problem. She was not required, or even permitted, to think for herself there. Though she was highly skilled at being a scrub nurse, she was allowed almost no autonomy. That had suited her when she was younger and willing to watch the decision-making exercised solely by the surgeons. But she was older now, and needed something more from her job.

In the OR she had scarcely interacted with the patients at all, except for a kind word, an encouraging smile. Seeing patients come onto the floor frightened and in pain, and knowing that she could help them psychologically adjust to their disease as well as provide services that could make a real physical difference, had special rewards for Judy. It was a privilege, being allowed to share in some of the most compelling moments of a person's life, where the very existence of that life was threatened.

Most doctors never shared this level of intimacy with their patients, despite their being the ones who directed care and controlled a patient's fate. It was the nurses who provided the necessary sympathy, the human-to-human empathy, on an hourly basis. Working on the floor with cancer patients was a demanding job emotionally and psychologically, as well as physically, but its satisfactions were commensurate. Getting older, or a growing maturity, had made this type of nursing more gratifying to her than the drama of the OR, Judy thought as she returned the chart to the rack.

Floor nursing required a wide variety of different skills. Her observations and assessments here were important. Judy had spent the past two years learning how to handle patients who started to go "bad," and gaining experience in dealing with the psychosocial aspects of seriously ill patients and their families. On the floor she felt she had a real influence on a patient's hospital course.

In addition, it took assurance and knowledge to work effectively with the staff physicians and the continually changing residents, who were often brusque and demanding. Sometimes interns and residents were even unjustly accusing because of their own need to be right, or their obvious exhaustion.

Occasionally, too, her fellow nurses seemed a hotbed of powerless groupies, pointing fingers at each other so they could satisfy the insistent doctors or feel that they had some power in their subordinate position. A few nurses even wanted to win points for themselves with a favorite potential partner. It was so easy to fall in love with a doctor when you admired his air of confidence, his indefatigable attempts to save a patient, his intelligence, and his bedside manner.

Judy knew precisely how that could happen. Once upon a time it had happened to her.

Andrea, her favorite nurse on the floor, stuck her head around the door. "Judy? Your patient in 12 just turned on his call light. Want me to get it for you?"

"No, thanks. I'm finished here." Judy secured the stethoscope around her neck and moved with her usual purposeful stride down the hall to 612 East.

* * *

Roger had not yet decided whether to get a new car. If he did, he knew he would go to an auto dealership and simply buy one he liked. That was how he did things, impulsively. None of this weeks of visiting different places and reading *Consumer Reports*. If he saw a car that he liked, he would buy it. Actually, he would have liked a red sports car, but it seemed inappropriate when he was in mourning.

When he arrived to pick up Judy and Liza, he felt rather conspicuous in the crumpled Audi. Though the car ran, the right front fender knocked noisily against the frame and there was a high-pitched whine that he didn't like one bit. As he climbed out of his car, he noticed the tall teenager standing near the front door of the building he was headed for. Roger inspected him with curiosity. He was a nice-looking boy, though not quite grown into his sharp features. His spiky brown hair was just long enough to aggravate a mother.

"Are you the doctor they're waiting for?" the boy asked, his gaze fixed on Roger's damaged car.

"Yes, I'm Roger Janek," he said. "You must be Larry."

"Must I?" Though the words could have been insolent, the tone was merely amused. The boy switched his gaze to Roger and took him in with frank interest. "Did you and Aunt Judy need a chaperon? Is that why Mom's going?"

Roger had reached the front door by now. Without

answering Larry's question, he rang the bell. He was several inches taller than the boy, whose brown eyes remained coolly skeptical as he observed Roger's unconscious mannerism of swinging his car keys around his forefinger.

"You nervous or what?" the boy asked.

"Why do you ask?"

"Because you keep swinging those keys like they're a toy. I thought only kids did things like that."

An interesting observation. Roger had seen a stream of youthful patients over the years, and sure enough the boys had often tapped their feet, snapped their fingers, drummed their fists on any available surface. Barely controlled energy, much as his was, he supposed. "You don't see other adults do it?" he asked.

"Hardly ever." Larry looked thoughtful. "Not at school, anyhow. Some of the women teachers are twittery, but not like that. Most of them have nerves of iron. You have to, in city schools."

The door opened behind Roger, and he turned with a smile. Judy's sister, standing beside her, bore a slight resemblance, but it wasn't striking. Liza had a gamin look about her, slightly fey, whereas Judy looked girl-next-door wholesome. The boy, when formally introduced, shook hands with Roger at his mother's urging.

"I could fix that rattle," he said suddenly.

Roger witnessed a moment of almost suspended

animation in his companions. Liza's frozen expression was worried, Judy's suspicious, and Larry's challengingly helpful. Roger caught the spinning car keys in a solid grip and considered. "What would you do?"

"I'd just wire it tight to the frame. It would mean making a little hole, but what difference would that make?"

What difference indeed? Roger was about to agree when Liza said, "It's probably not a good idea, Larry. You don't have the tools."

"Mike has everything I'd need, and I know he's home." He shrugged with apparent indifference. "Hey, I was just trying to be useful. Never mind."

Roger looked questioningly at Liza, who indicated her uncertainty. Well, he was here to try to help the boy, and what better track to get off on than trusting him? "Okay," he agreed, tossing over the keys. "But I don't want you driving around in the car."

"I'll have to just run it a few feet to see if the rattle's gone."

"Just on the block, okay?"

"Sure. No problem." And Larry was off down the sidewalk at a jog.

"You're too trusting," Judy murmured.

"Do you think I shouldn't have done it?" he asked.

"I really don't know. Shall we take my car?"

Roger found it strangely relaxing to hear the sisters squabble good-naturedly about which Chinese restaurant was the best in the neighborhood, and then, seated opposite him, about which dishes they would order. Liza struck him as less mature than Judy, but a pleasant, well-meaning woman. She had hair several shades lighter than her sister's and wore it in a longer style. She was altogether different than Judy, too, in her way of speaking, which was quick and breathy and seldom straight to the point. Judy's voice had a certain gravelly melody, which she enhanced by talking with her hands and eyes, as well.

"Has Larry always gotten into trouble?" Roger asked, to get the ball rolling.

Liza's shoulders hunched almost protectively. "It always seemed to me he was no more naughty than the next kid, when he was young—five, six. Later he became more of a handful. He was really fond of his dad, and they did all kinds of things together—fishing, playing sports, going to fairs and amusement parks. Bob was pretty much able to manage him. More than me, anyhow. But since his father died, Larry hasn't been the same. Even when we were still in the valley, he started to act up more at school. I thought it would be a good idea to start fresh somewhere else, but it's only gotten worse in San Francisco."

Judy sighed. "You have to understand, Roger, that it's not as if he flatly refuses to do most things. He just pretty much does what he wants to instead, as if you hadn't said anything. He's like that in school, too, which causes a lot of problems."

"And at the sports club," Liza said. "Even though he used to really like basketball and stuff."

Roger helped himself to a bowl of wonton soup. "Give me an example."

Liza grimaced. "We had a call from the sports club just last week. They said Larry had been warned that he'd be asked not to come there if he didn't put back the weights he used. It's as if he won't take on any responsibility he doesn't choose to, big or small."

"Did he take on responsibility before your husband died?"

Liza frowned in thought. "Well, he'd do things, but you had to really insist. Like usually Bob kind of bribed him, you know? 'If you clean up your room, I'll take you to the county fair.' That kind of thing."

Roger looked questioningly at Judy. "Is that how you saw it, too?"

"I was only around occasionally when Larry was growing up. You see, Bob was still a bit of an adolescent at heart," she said, flashing an apologetic look at her sister. "He was a wonderful guy, but he couldn't be very firm with the boy. He *liked* to play basketball with Larry and his friends, or take them horseback riding, so he didn't lay down the law the way some fathers do. They were like buddies, Bob and Larry."

Liza nodded. "They were. When Bob died, Larry

lost both his father and his friend. I couldn't begin to make up for that, as much as I wanted to."

"Nor has Liza ever been the world's greatest disciplinarian," Judy offered, pressing her sister's hand. "She's very softhearted. And now it's especially hard to make Larry do things he doesn't want to, because we know how unhappy he is."

"I can understand that." Roger, his brows drawn together in thought, ladled each of them another serving of wonton soup. "Tell me. How would you like Larry to be different? What would you like for him?"

Liza rested her chin on her knuckles, her eyes becoming dreamy. "I'd want him to be happy. Even when he's doing things he chooses, he doesn't seem content. I'd want him to help around the flat, to pick up his room and do dishes and finish his homework."

Judy added, "And I'd want him to find wholesome things to do where he felt a sense of accomplishment. I'd want him to care about his future, instead of acting like there's nothing beyond today."

"I'd like him to care about me." Liza's pixie face flushed. "Maybe that's asking too much of a teenager."

Judy said, "He cares about you, Liza. He's just wrapped up in himself right now."

"Is Larry interested in girls?" Roger asked.

"We don't know," Liza admitted. "He doesn't talk about them, but sometimes he gets calls from girls."

Roger pushed the bowl of steamed rice in Judy's direction, and she smiled at him. She had quite a startling smile, full of mischievous good humor, which Roger hadn't actually noticed before. Her eyes sparkled, and the generous curve of her lips twitched with a warm amusement.

"We're hoping a girl will come along and be the making of him," she teased. "You know, that softening, civilizing influence that women have provided through the centuries."

Roger returned her rueful look and set down the chopsticks he was expertly wielding on a diced chicken dish. "In the meantime I'll see if I can civilize him in a different way. Maybe do the things divorced fathers do with their teenagers—take him to movies, maybe a ball game when he's past his popcorn phase, even drive him to visit some colleges if he'd like. Once I get to know what he's interested in it will be easier. Does he play tennis?"

Liza shook her head. "Not that I know of, anyway."

"Of course," Roger concluded, "all this depends on whether he likes me enough to spend time with me."

"He will," Liza said fervently. "This will be just what he needs."

But Larry wasn't on Twenty-second Avenue when they returned, nor was Roger's Audi. Liza looked mortified, Judy grim. It had been two hours since they left for dinner. Roger suggested that Liza check to see if Mike was home, but she returned with the news that Larry's friend wasn't there, either. So much for trusting the kid, Roger thought. "Let's go inside and see if there's a message," he suggested.

The flat into which the sisters led him was a typical upper unit in a Victorian building, with a railway arrangement of the rooms off of one long hall. There was a bedroom over the stairs and then another room, typically used as a living room but serving as another bedroom in this household.

Liza pointed to the room over the stairs. "That's Larry's bedroom, but if he's left a message it will be in the kitchen."

There was a plant-strewn split bath on the right, and the last room on the left served as the family-living room, with TV, sofa, and chairs. The kitchen was large, a cheerful room with white-painted wood cabinets and a table surrounded by four chairs. Judy frowned as she checked the notepad and the answering machine. "Nothing. I'm afraid he's just gone off with it, Roger. I'm sorry."

"Did his friend's parents know where they'd gone?" he asked.

Liza shook her head. "They don't seem to pay much attention to Mike. It's one of the things that makes him such a bad companion for Larry."

"I'll put on some water for coffee," Judy offered.

"Maybe you could wait awhile before you do

something," Liza said hopefully. "He'll probably be back soon."

This proved to be too optimistic a forecast. When Roger had been there an hour, with each of them traveling regularly to the front window to look out into the street, he said it might be wise for them to call the police. Liza blanched, and Judy determinedly looked away.

"It's not just the car," Roger explained. "He knew we'd be back, and he probably had every intention of getting here before we did. If he isn't here by now, maybe he's in trouble."

There was just the barest pause before Judy nodded. "Of course. Use the phone in my room."

While he made the call, his eyes wandered over the wicker furniture and brightly colored pillows. The bedspread had great splashes of green, red, blue, and yellow in vaguely flower-like patterns. There were several white wicker bookshelves, looking less than durable but successfully holding a wide array of books—nursing texts, mysteries, biographies, computer manuals. On any bare surfaces were either vases with silk flowers or frames with multiple pictures in them. It was a cheerful room with the subtle fragrance of vanilla.

When he had finished making the call, he found that Judy and Liza had moved from the kitchen to the living room at the back of the flat. It was a quiet space, with beige carpeting and a brown corduroy-covered sofa. "They'll keep an eye out for the car," he said, remaining near the door. "I gave them my home number as well as this one, so I think I'll just go back there."

Judy started to wiggle her feet into a pair of tennis shoes. "I'll drive you."

Just as the two of them were descending the stairs, the doorbell rang. Through the marbled glass at the top of the door, Roger could see three figures, one taller with a familiarly shaped hat. Judy winced and called back up the stairs to her sister, "I think the police are here, Liza, with the boys."

Chapter Four

Liza almost instantly appeared at the head of the stairs. "Make sure he's okay, Judy. Before anything else."

Judy pulled open the door to display a ruddy-faced young policeman, Larry, and a boy about his age. Larry looked more pained than defiant, which was the other boy's obvious emotion. The policeman said, "I'm Officer Cragon. Are you this boy's mother?" He laid a hand possessively on Larry's shoulder.

"His aunt, but that's his mother upstairs. Are you all right, Larry?"

"Yeah. I'm okay."

"Let's try to sort this out," the officer suggested. Turning to Roger, he said, "Was it your car, sir?"

"Yes. But I just called it in. That's awfully fast work."

"We'd already picked the kids up," he replied. "I heard the APB on the radio on the way over here."

Judy frowned. "How did you know the kids shouldn't have had the car?"

The policeman laughed. "Actually, I'd stopped to help them. But they acted so self-conscious about it that I was suspicious. This one," he said, tapping Larry's shoulder, "said the car had already been smashed up. Is that true?"

"Yes. But it was running last time I saw it," Roger said regretfully.

"Well, it's not now," Officer Cragon said.

"It was that whine," Larry complained. "I didn't do anything to it. The whine just got louder and louder until—blam!—something gave and the car just stopped. It would have happened with you in it."

"Probably," Roger agreed. "Of course, if the whine got louder, I would automatically have pulled over. Not that it would have made much difference."

"I was going to, when it happened," Larry admitted. "Look, don't blame it on Mike, sir. He just came along for the ride. I talked him into it."

Liza, who had arrived down at the bottom of the stairs, looked skeptical but said nothing. The policeman looked questioningly at Roger, with the comment, "It's up to you, Doctor. He wasn't in the car when I stopped, so it would be a little difficult to charge him."

Roger hesitated, and then nodded. "Sure. He's really not my problem. But I would suggest, Judy, that you make his parents aware of what happened."

His eyes held a challenge, and Judy said, "Certainly. I'll call them when we have this settled."

Officer Cragon nodded dismissal to Mike, who was unwise enough to laugh with teenage mockery at the impotence of the law. "I'll keep my eye out for you, son," the policeman said, with amiable threat in his voice.

Then he suggested that the rest of them go upstairs to talk. Liza looked warily at Roger and muttered something at her son, which Roger couldn't hear. Judy led the procession up the carpeted stairs and back to the family room for their conference. Larry took a seat on the sofa between his mother and his aunt.

It was impossible for Roger to tell what the boy was thinking or how he was feeling from the determinedly bland cast of his face. Roger and the policeman drew the two other chairs closer to the sofa, and there was a pause before the policeman scratched his head and indicated Larry with his chin.

"When I stopped to help, this one was behind the wheel and the other one was doing something at the engine with the hood up. There was a haze of smoke or exhaust still hovering around the car, and I thought they were just having trouble getting it going. Larry was perfectly calm about my arrival, but the other one, Mike, seemed very edgy. Which led to my asking about the registration."

"Where were they?" Roger asked.

"On the Great Highway."

Roger turned to the boy. "Where were you going with it? I don't imagine you thought you could steal it."

"We were just driving it, checking to see if it still rattled, and what the whine was. We were . . . I was going to bring it back. Honest."

"The thing is," the policeman interposed, "you'd given the kid permission to work on it, right?"

"Yes, with specific instructions that he not take it off the block."

"Rather trusting," Officer Cragon pronounced, observing Roger dubiously. "You know the kid well?"

"No, I just met him, but I know Judy, who's his aunt. I wanted to show Larry that I trusted him."

The policeman narrowed intent brown eyes. "Why?"

"God knows," Roger muttered. He could tell from the officer's expression that he thought Roger had done it somehow to impress Judy, but he wasn't prepared to argue with the man's perception. "What happens now?"

"That depends on you. The kid took the car when he wasn't supposed to, and in spite of your showing all that trust in him. I can arrest him if you'll file a complaint."

"And what would happen to him?"

Officer Cragon shrugged. "He'd appear in juvenile court and be meted out some kind of justice. Under the circumstances, that would probably be community service rather than detention at juvenile hall. I mean, because you gave him permission to drive the car, and because kids are usually charged with joyriding rather than stealing cars."

Everyone in the room was watching Roger closely. "Well, I think I ought to do it," he said.

Judy and Liza looked incredulous, and Larry's face paled. Roger switched his gaze to the officer and kept it level with earnestness. "It's a matter of principle," he said. "Kids have to learn to take responsibility for their actions. You let them get away with something, like we just did with his friend Mike, and he's going to think he can get away with it anytime he wants."

"But I wouldn't!" Larry protested.

Liza and Judy said nothing.

Officer Cragon seemed to have caught on. "I agree with you. It's sobering for kids to learn that there are real consequences to their actions. The juvenile court will appoint an attorney for him and provide a defense."

"And how many hours of community service would he be likely to get?"

"Oh, hard to say. It would depend on the judge. Some of them are soft and some of them are pretty tough. Maybe a hundred hours," he said, and Roger, with the hand out of sight of the sisters, motioned upward, "and maybe twice that," the officer continued. "But the experience would be unforgettable for a middle-class kid. He'd think twice before he did something like that again, I promise you."

"Roger." Judy was leaning toward him with a determined set to her jaw. "You knew enough about Larry that you might have guessed what would happen. It's almost as much your fault as it is his. He didn't hurt the car. It was already a mess and would have broken down if you'd been driving it, too. Maybe you could show him a little leniency."

"Yes, please," Liza added. "He didn't really mean to do any harm."

"Well," the policeman said, "that's how a lot of them start out, you know. They don't mean anything. Then it starts to look real easy, and they think they're smarter than anyone else, see? Pretty soon they're acting like they're outside the law." He frowned at Larry. "I'm sure you're a good kid, but getting you off without punishment just isn't really smart. The doctor would be doing you a favor."

"That's what I think, too," Roger said. "Community service won't do him any harm."

"But maybe he won't get community service," Judy pointed out. "Maybe they'll lock him up in juvenile hall to teach him a lesson. Or send him to some group home or something. It's a terrible risk to take."

Roger gnawed at his lip. "There is that. What do you suggest?"

Liza and Judy looked at each other. Larry looked hopefully at them and then down at the floor. The young policeman cleared his throat. "I have an idea."

They each looked at him, all but Roger not very hopefully.

"Probably the doctor here could supervise the kid for the two hundred hours. Get him doing some volunteer work at the hospital, maybe working around his house or something. If you wanted to trust the kid around your house," he added. "You could sign some kind of contract. If Larry fulfills his end of the bargain, I'll amend my report to show that. Of course, it means a lot of work for the doctor. Maybe he wouldn't be willing to do that."

They all switched their gazes to Roger. "Well, I guess I'd consider it," he said. "How about you, Larry?"

"Seems like a hundred hours would be more reasonable," the teenager bargained.

His mother groaned. "Don't look a gift horse in the mouth, Larry."

"Hundred and fifty," Roger suggested.

Larry hesitated, and then nodded. "Okay. I'm not real big on manual labor, though."

"I'll try to bear that in mind," Roger said, with a wink at Judy when the others were rising to conclude the transaction. She didn't acknowledge his signal, and he sighed inwardly. Maybe it was better that she didn't understand he had manipulated the situation to achieve this result. He had just been given a bit of authority in Larry's life, something he couldn't have achieved very easily under the circumstances he had himself proposed.

Officer Cragon talked quietly with him in the hallway while the others were drafting a two-line contract for Larry and Roger to sign. "I hope this is what you wanted," he said with a grin. "Better you than me. Teenagers are both confused and confusing."

"You couldn't have done better if we'd rehearsed it." Roger shook his hand firmly. "I may call you for advice."

"I hope I'll be able to give you some." The policeman turned to leave, but paused to add, "He seems like an okay kid, really. Good luck."

"Thanks. I imagine I'll need it."

It had been an emotionally exhausting evening for Judy. When the car was missing, she had felt ashamed of her nephew, and a little angry that Roger had insisted on trusting the boy. Hadn't this whole thing come about because Roger knew the boy had been getting into trouble? And yet it had been a hopeful gesture on Roger's part, and might have worked well if Larry hadn't acted irresponsibly.

Then, when the policeman had arrived, she'd felt

a panic set in. What if her nephew were to get caught up in the juvenile legal system, treated like a hardened criminal? It wasn't all that unrealistic a fear, from the stories one heard. Larry was far too naive and inexperienced to be thrown in with treacherous youngsters.

When the neighbor Mike had been released, she had felt a great sense of relief, thinking the same would happen with Larry. Judy had felt angry with Roger when he insisted on signing a complaint. Certainly, Roger was right that her nephew should be held liable for his actions, but couldn't he imagine how things could go wrong at a juvenile hearing? He had supposedly come here to *help* the boy.

Now, in a sense, they were adversaries, and she'd hoped they'd be friends. She had wanted to see him laugh again, as he used to before Kerri died. She remembered him then as a lighthearted, teasing young man, ready for a party, like most of the overworked doctors. Once, when she was still in the OR before transferring to the floor, he had told a story during surgery of a man and his shaggy dog that had almost brought the operation to a standstill, everyone was laughing so hard. That was a long time ago now.

Liza paused at Judy's open door before going to bed. "You think it will work out okay, don't you?"

Judy looked up from the computer manual she was studying. "Sure. Roger isn't going to be a slave driver. I'm sure he still just wants to straighten Larry out."

"I suppose." Liza sighed. "I didn't expect him to agree to press charges. That didn't seem very nice of him."

"No, it didn't. But he agreed to the contract in the end. I'm just hoping Larry won't make a fuss about that, once he's had to work for a while."

"I know. That worries me, too. You don't suppose Roger would go back to the police if Larry balks, do you?"

Judy's mouth twisted ruefully. "I'm not sure he wouldn't, Liza. Actually, when you get right down to it, I don't know him all that well."

"Yeah. Well, we'll just hope for the best." Liza rubbed a weary hand over her face. "I'm exhausted."

"You and me." Judy put aside the computer manual and rose. "I'm going to bed."

"Me, too. Things will look better in the morning."

Judy wasn't so sure, but she did remember just then that Roger had winked at her. What had that been about?

Roger had a strange, disturbing dream that night. He was in the mountains, at the cabin. Kerri was there, though he couldn't see her. And their room was decorated differently, with white wicker furniture and color-splashed bedspread and pillows. There was a small dog, getting into mischief, chewing on socks, and running off after mysterious animals. Roger knew that Kerri wanted him to train the dog, but it had ruined his favorite shoes and he'd lost patience.

"You can get another pair of shoes," Kerri's voice said, but he still couldn't see her.

"Dogs aren't always trainable," he insisted.

"You can train them if you're patient and you love them," her disembodied voice said.

"Where are you?" Roger asked. "I can't see you."

"I'm right here behind you," she said. But when he turned there was no one there, just the dog, cowering from him as though he'd hit it.

And then the scene changed and he was in the OR, but instead of being the anesthesiologist he was the surgeon doing the operating. A scalpel had materialized in his hand when he simply thought that he needed one. No nurse had handed it to him, because there was no nurse in the room. In fact, there was no one in the room except himself and the patient, lying there with his belly sliced open and the viscera starting to throb their way out of the abdominal cavity.

Roger knew he had to work quickly, but he didn't know what he was expected to do. Everything looked perfectly normal to him. There was no massive tumor obvious or inflamed section of intestine. And the body parts were oozing up through the incision and out onto the Betadined skin around the opening.

"What should I do?" he asked, though the patient

was unconscious and there was no one else to answer him.

The loudspeaker on the wall intoned in his father's voice, "First things first. Are your hands clean?"

"Of course they are," he said impatiently, but he looked down and they weren't. They were ungloved and covered with mud. He knew he would have to scrub them, but the viscera continued to slither through the bloody slit and there wasn't time. "I don't have time to clean them," he cried.

"There's always time to do the right thing," the voice intoned, and then it laughed and laughed, until the operating room rang with the sound.

Roger woke to the laughter of a DJ on the radio. Blinking uncertainly at the source of this noise, he saw that it was six o'clock, and he groaned. He felt like he'd been run over by a truck, and he pulled himself wearily out of his solitary king-size bed and stumbled toward the shower.

Chapter Five

Judy knew that Roger had been in touch with Larry, and that the boy had spent several hours at Roger's house one evening when she was at her computer class. But her schedule had not coincided very well with her sister's or her nephew's, and she didn't know precisely what was happening on the "community service" scene. So she was wary when Roger appeared at her side as she walked toward her car after a Saturday shift at Fielding.

"I wonder if you'd give me a ride home, and we could talk," he said.

"Sure. You haven't replaced the car yet?"

Roger shrugged. "Not yet. I borrowed a friend's car for a few days."

So where is it, Judy wanted to ask, but held her tongue. If he asked for a ride, she was going to give him a ride. If that meant he was leaving his car in the Fielding parking garage, that was his problem. She unlocked the passenger door of the Civic and walked around to the driver's side as he climbed in and reached over to unlock her door. He looked tired, slumped down against the seat of her car.

"How about if we forget we have any problems for an hour or so?" she suggested. "Let me take you out to dinner, and we'll talk and laugh and just be friends from the hospital for a while."

"Judy, it's only four-thirty."

"Okay, so we'll play miniature golf first. Do you like miniature golf?"

"Well, I . . ." Roger paused, and apparently revised what he was going to say. "Yes, but there aren't any courses around here like we used to play back East. They're all artificial turf with boring angles instead of little houses and fairy-tale scenarios."

"I know where there's an old-fashioned one."

Roger looked skeptical. "We've . . . I've never found one. The Malibu Grand Prix isn't like that, or the one near Santa Rosa. Besides, even those are too far."

Judy pursed her lips. "Mine's a little farther. Maybe an hour and a half." She watched his reaction, a reluctant interest. "But it's fun, with a dinosaur and a Humpty-Dumpty and a big fish you shoot the ball through."

"We have to talk about Larry eventually."

"Sure, but later. I've had a hard week, Roger. Not

just at home. Two of my patients have died painful deaths, my supervisor has decided we all need to do more paperwork, and I got a needle stick because some resident left a needle under a gauze pad. Not an AIDS patient, fortunately, but a lot of hassle. Tell me how Nan LeBaron and Steve Winstead managed to find each other, and I'll tell you about Dr. Parker's latest investment scheme—in leeches. Just for a few hours let's enjoy ourselves."

"Barney's investing in leeches?" Roger asked.

Taking this as acceptance of her proposition, Judy swung the car toward the Golden Gate Bridge. "You know how they've been touting them for after microsurgery. He bought half of a leech farm in England. Honest to God. And he's trying to get all of us to come in with him, by showing us the most disgusting pictures of these bloated black slugs."

Judy found, not to her surprise, that Roger loved hearing what everyone was up to. He'd kept himself apart from hospital happenings for the past year and had a lot of catching up to do. But he had his share of information to impart, being close friends with several people who had intrigued the medical center during the past year. Judy rolled down her window to catch the warm afternoon breeze as they sped up Route 101 through Marin County. She began to relax, something she felt she hadn't done in a long time.

"Tell me the shaggy dog story," she said. "I remember it was hilarious, but I don't recall how it ended."

"You remember that?" Roger smiled reminiscently. "I bet I haven't told that story in two years, and I used to tell it to everyone new I met."

As they rolled northward and he told the silly shaggy dog story for her, including its most outrageous embellishments and impossibly bad puns and exaggerations, his eyes sparkled with enjoyment. Judy laughed until tears came to her eyes. At Cotati, she turned off the highway, explaining that she liked the drive through Sebastopol.

"We can come back the other way, if you like. I don't think it's actually any faster."

He tugged at an ear and smiled. "I'm not in any hurry."

"Good. We'll play both courses."

When they arrived at the Pee-Wee golf course, just across the bridge from Guerneville, Judy turned a mischievous face to him. "I'm really good at this, Roger. I'm just warning you so your male ego won't get crushed if I beat the pants off you."

"Hey, I'm not bad at miniature golf, either." He glanced around him, taking in the large green dinosaur and the flower pots full of impatiens. "You know, I don't think I've ever even been to the Russian River. When I have time off, I go to our cabin in the mountains."

Judy could tell the thought brought memories of

Kerri, and she quickly shepherded him toward the counter where golf clubs were laid out. "I want a red ball. They're always lucky for me. No, I'm paying. This is all my treat."

"I don't see why it should be," he objected.

But Judy merely shook her head and pulled a twenty-dollar bill from her wallet. "You can keep score, if you like."

Judy was in the white slacks and pastel shirt that served as a uniform for many of the nurses at Fielding. Since she'd played the course before, she offered to lead off.

"With the 'Old Grist Mill' you try to put it through the center hole, but if you go off the side, you end up okay, too." She tapped her red ball smartly, and it sailed down the path and through the mill. It slowed slightly as it rolled out the other side—and into the hole.

"A hole in one on the first hole," she crowed, doing a little victory dance. "Just try to beat that, Roger Janek!"

Roger was in slacks and a sport shirt, and he wore comfortable-looking deck shoes that he lined up with his putter as he tapped his green ball just a little too hard. The ball sailed up the path and smacked into the rotting miniature grist mill, flipping back toward him and rolling back to exactly where it had started.

"Too bad," Judy teased, "but not all of us can be experts. You'll hit your stride."

"And when I do, I won't mock you," he grumbled.

"Oh, sure you will."

And he did, because that became the pattern as they worked their way through the delightful course. Roger did better on the catapult and the castle, but Judy came back on "Cwazy Wabbit."

"Don't you just love their names?" she asked. "I've always wanted to have a miniature golf course. I'd design the little buildings and the traps, and I'd give them all names that were puns. Actually, you could use puns from the shaggy dog story and build a whole course around that."

Together they devised their own course as they played, making wild plans for extravagant palaces and excessive punning names for the holes, until Roger was laughing and Judy was feeling almost light-headed, as though she'd been drinking champagne or breathing nitrous oxide. The scent of the flowers and the beauty of cool redwoods around them were intoxicating. Being released from the city, and from the hospital, and from her worries about her sister and her nephew was doing wonders for her.

Judy grinned across at Roger as his ball was hit by the "black widow spider" just when it was about to plop into the hole.

"What a pity!" she cried. "Oh, poor Roger. Better luck next time, fella!"

Judy won the front course handily, but Roger had

been getting better as they went along. The back course, complete with a cannibal scene of a native in a pot, was almost as unfamiliar to Judy as to her companion. Here he began to take his revenge on her, to concentrate on his putting and control the force with which he sent his balls off on the first stroke of each hole.

He was suspiciously gallant as his scores began to better hers, and she saw the gleam get brighter in his eyes. He tugged at a belt loop as he watched her try several times to project her ball into position to sink it. "Have you had your eyes checked recently?" he asked with feigned concern. "No one with good eyesight could have missed that shot."

"Why, you little snail!" she laughed, remembering his fascination with "escargot" on the previous course. "Some of us aren't here to compete. We're just playing for the fun of it."

"Oh, sure, like that's what you've been up to all afternoon," he said. "Mocking me and laughing when I went out of bounds. Serves you right."

He looked adorable standing there, leaning on his putter, his smile full of good humor and . . . well, he looked happy. That was all she could think of to describe him just then. Sunlight seemed to catch in his curly brown hair like a halo. His face, so unusually carefree, seemed particularly endearing. There were stray hairs in his eyebrows that shot off in odd directions. There was a patch of stubble high up on his left cheek where he'd missed shaving that morning.

Seeing him so cheerful, Judy realized that Roger was meant to be a happy man. He was meant to enjoy life and get the most from it. Which was why he'd been so confused and hurt by his Kerri's death. He didn't quite know how to cope with a life in which he was diminished by tragedy, weighed down by grief. It would be a pleasure to see him regain his balance. Judy hoped today meant he was working his way toward happier times.

They squabbled like kids over who was going to add up the scores at the end of the second round, each accusing the other of not being reliable. When they had both had a turn, and found that they tied, Judy grinned at him and said, "See? I knew I could teach you how to play."

"Ha! You were going to beat the pants off me. You just didn't know how good I'd be once I got the hang of it again."

"Some people just can't help but brag," she scoffed. "I'm starved. I know a great place for dinner in Monte Rio where we can sit outside near the river."

"Lead on." Roger deposited their putters on the counter, stuffed the scorecard in the back pocket of his slacks, and caught up with her at the Civic.

* * *

The day's heat had begun to dissipate by the time they were shown to a table on the terraces overlooking the Russian River. Roger felt remarkably serene sitting back in his chair and watching the water flow down toward the bridge. In the back of his mind he knew it was easier to be here because he had no associations with Kerri at the Russian River, but in the foreground he allowed himself to simply enjoy the ease with which he and Judy could talk, mostly about Fielding and the people they knew there.

Because of a hillside of redwoods, the sun had already vanished from the terraces, but the lanterns strung above the tables created a festive atmosphere. Judy had ordered a dark beer, and Roger had ordered a glass of white wine. They touched glasses, and each offered a frivolous toast: "To the finer points of miniature golf," Judy said; "To the perfect spot for eating a rare steak," Roger suggested.

"With mushrooms and herb butter. Sounds good to me, too."

"They have pasta and fish. All kinds of healthy choices," he teased. "Of course, you've already broken one health law. Your nose is sunburned."

"Is it?" She tapped it gingerly with her index finger. "It can't be very bad, if it doesn't hurt when I touch it."

"No, just enough to give it a healthy glow. And

your cheeks, too. Don't you get out in the sun much?"

"Unlike some of us, I am *not* a health nut," she retorted. "I don't ski in the winter, or swim in the summer, or play tennis or racquetball, or ride a bike, or any of those wholesome things. I'm a slug."

He regarded her with amusement. "You don't look like a slug. Don't you like sports?"

"Not much." She wrinkled her nose. "Miniature golf is about my speed. And I walk."

"Yeah? A lot?"

Judy reached down and lifted a pedometer from her waist. "About forty miles, since Monday."

"Really? When do you do it?"

"Oh, whenever I can, or whenever I have to. I put in a lot of miles at work. And most days I walk from the flat to Fielding and back. Or I walk at lunchtime. It all adds up."

They paused in their discussion to give their order to the waiter, but Roger was intrigued enough to pick up the thread. "How long have you been wearing the pedometer?"

"Several years. I didn't put on nearly as many miles when I worked in the OR."

Roger looked thoughtful. "I remember you in the OR. You were amazingly efficient and good-natured. Everyone was surprised, and disappointed, when you decided to switch to floor nursing. Why did you do that?"

Judy shrugged. "Oh, just for a change of pace, I guess."

"I doubt that. My guess would be that you had a very good reason. The surgeons at Fielding didn't give you a hard time, did they?"

"Nothing I couldn't handle."

Roger cocked his head at her. "Obviously you don't intend to tell me the whole story. Well, there's no reason you should. You just always seem so blunt and forthright." He waved aside the comment. "Sorry. I meant it as a compliment, not a criticism. And I didn't say it to get you to tell me something you want to keep private. I'm a bit blunt myself. People don't always like it."

"I do. But it *is* something personal and kind of a downer, and we're here to enjoy ourselves." Judy reached across to briefly touch his hand. "I'm going to tell you about Randy McCracken's spiritual enlightenment, which is a much more interesting story."

Roger watched her animated face, her extravagantly gesticulating hands, and the energetic stillness of her body. She was a study in contrasts. On the surface she radiated lightness and enthusiasm, but this seemed to be underpinned with a more complex nature. And her view of things had an intriguing originality. Calling Randy's adventure with a gypsy contingent in the ICU waiting room a "spiritual enlightenment" suggested an offbeat personal vision, to which Roger responded instinctively.

Her eyes, a deep shade of blue, were wide and expressive. She met his gaze almost constantly, with none of the wandering discomfort that so many people exhibited. There was even the promise of openness—on another occasion. She didn't seem so much reluctant to tell him her story, as to avoid it today, when they were playing with only happy memories.

He hadn't laughed in too long. It was almost like unused muscles, these neglected humor reservoirs of his. At first it felt strange, hearing himself laughing, telling jokes. His grief had denied him the ability, and almost the right, to feel happy. But he *did* feel happy, right now in the failing daylight with the river flowing past below them. He enjoyed making Judy laugh. She had such a warm, bubbling laugh, especially when she was surprised into amusement. It had been a great idea to get away for a few hours.

Unfortunately, when they returned to Judy's car, the left rear tire was flat. "No problem," she said. "I've got a spare."

But when they opened her trunk, it was bare. Judy ground her teeth in frustration. "That little jerk has really done it now! He promised me, he absolutely *promised* me, that he'd put it back in before the day was out. Why didn't I check it to make sure? I know how he is. But he talked about buying the new tire for Liza's car, and why the hell wouldn't he have put mine back then? How lazy and irresponsible can you get? I'd like to strangle the little toad."

"I presume we're talking about Larry," Roger guessed, grinning.

"Who else? I'm sorry, Roger. I'll call Triple A."

But the automobile club had several emergencies and couldn't even estimate when they might be able to reach Judy in Monte Rio. Discouraged, she stepped out of the phone booth to find Roger checking his watch. It was already after ten, and Judy apologized again. "I haven't had any trouble with it in so long, I'd almost forgotten this could happen," she said unhappily.

"Don't worry about it." He nodded toward the bar across the room from the phone booth. "We'll just have a drink while we wait."

The bartender, a young man with long blond hair, leaned toward Judy and said, "I wouldn't bank on their getting here anytime soon. There's only one truck for a huge area. Saturday night sometimes they don't show up till the middle of the night."

Judy groaned. "Well, I don't see what else we can do."

The young man, who obviously mistook them for a couple, suggested, "There was a cancellation for one of the rooms. You could just spend the night and take care of everything in the morning."

She laughed. "No, I don't think that would work."

"Why not?" Roger tugged absently at his watch-band. "You could call your sister and tell her you'll be back tomorrow so she won't worry."

"Roger, they only have one room." She turned to the bartender. "Twin beds, by any chance?"

Puzzled, he shook his head. "No, it's an antique brass bed, really neat. All the rooms are done up with antiques. They only have a few they rent out, and they all share this one great old bathroom, so it's not very expensive. Especially for bed and breakfast."

Roger said, "Let's do it. Otherwise, Judy, we're going to be really frustrated, and it will spoil the whole day. Tomorrow we can take care of things without the annoyance."

"But we don't have anything with us, and it sounds like just a double bed."

"We're grown-ups. We can handle it." At her worried frown he said, "Even if Triple A came in an hour or two, it would be the middle of the night before we got back to San Francisco."

Reluctantly, Judy agreed.

Chapter Six

They were shown upstairs to a lovely room overlooking the river. The Victorian furnishings were lush in color and fabric, rich red velvet curtains and red silk lamp shades. A basket of rose petal potpourri delicately scented the room, and there was a cushioned window seat in the area overlooking the water. Roger looked across at her, a question in his eyes, and she nodded. He said they'd take the room.

When the proprietor had left, Judy tried to apologize again, but Roger waved aside her protests. "Hey, it's not your fault. One of the things I've learned over the years is to just accept what happens and get on with your life. Well, maybe I haven't done that so well about Kerri, but it was my motto up until then. Why don't you give Triple A and your sister a call?"

There was no phone in the room, so she disappeared out the door and Roger caught sight of himself in the mirror above the miniature sink. His own face had gotten some sun, and he looked healthier than he had in a while. Jerry had told him he should spend more time out of doors, as he had when he worked in the yard at Nan's place. Obediently, Roger had plunged into checking out the flower beds in the rear yard of his Laurel Heights Victorian. But most of the work, and most of the May weather, had been enjoyed by the same Basque gardener who had done it for years, and who knew how to do it properly.

Now, seeing himself in the mirror, he liked feeling this alive. He liked seeing color in his face, experiencing a carefree happiness, and not feeling guilty for enjoying himself. Jerry would be proud of him, and Angel. Everyone was starting to urge him to do more, to let go of the deep sorrow that had held him down for so long. He just hadn't known it was possible, until tonight. He hadn't realized he could be so lighthearted and have fun again. Obviously, he was getting better.

Judy returned and laid the key on the dresser as she ran her fingers through her short, curly hair. "All taken care of. Liza said she'd drive up here in the morning with the tire Larry put in her car if we have any trouble getting hold of one on a Sunday. I said I'd let her know."

"I'm sure we'll manage." Roger hopped up on the high bed to test it out. "A little hard. I'm not as fond of hard beds as most people. But it will do."

Judy nodded, looking around the room as though something were missing. Well, most everything was missing, since they had no nightclothes or toothbrushes, and no way to get them, even if there were a store open this late.

Roger said, "Why don't you use the bathroom first? Then you can get in bed while I'm out of the room?"

By the time he returned from his trip to the massive old bathroom with its claw-footed tub and its heated towel rail, Judy had turned off the overhead light and only one of the red-shaded lamps still glowed in the room. She had taken the far side of the bed and lay facing the other direction. Roger slipped off his pants and shirt before climbing into the bed beside her. The bed was narrower than he had expected and even though Judy was as far as possible over on her side, there was not a great deal of distance between them.

"Are you ready for me to turn the light out?" he asked.

"Sure." In the ensuing dark she said, "This is so weird. I hope you don't mind too much."

"Not at all." Which wasn't entirely accurate. It wasn't so much that he minded as that he was intensely aware of her presence so close to him. He knew she would be in her bra and underpants, little bits of cloth separating herself from nakedness, and only inches separating her from him.

Roger found himself wondering what her compact, energetic body would look like. He loved the look of women's bodies, loved the amazing variety of their breasts and the rounded contours of their buttocks. He loved to see them naked in motion, walking up a pair of stairs before him or lifting something down from a shelf. He was not shy of his own body, and he appreciated it when a woman was able to walk naked around a room with no self-consciousness.

"Good night, Roger. Thanks for being such a good sport."

"Good night, Judy. Sleep well."

The first time he woke in the night, he found himself turned facing her, his body spooned against hers. He quickly moved back from her, chagrined at his unconscious behavior. Not that it was so bad to have responded to the warmth of another human body in the bed. It was almost natural. Roger rolled over to lie facing away from his companion, as far to his side of the bed as possible.

The next time he woke up, he found himself again pressed against his companion. This time his body was aroused, and he had an erection that strained against his shorts somewhere between Judy's legs. He was so distressed that he abruptly withdrew, accidentally kicking her as he did so.

Her hesitant voice whispered, "Roger?"

"Jesus Christ, I'm sorry, Judy. Honestly, I was

asleep and I didn't know what was happening until I woke up. You must think I'm some kind of pervert. I'll sleep on the floor."

"Don't be silly. It was just one of those things that happen." Her voice hesitated. "It just surprised me."

They lay as far apart as possible in the dark room, aware of each other but not speaking for a long time. Roger wondered how long she'd been awake before he woke, what she had thought when he pressed against her and became hard. She must have been a little frightened, or at the very least confused.

"I haven't, you know, been with anyone since Kerri died," he said finally into the blackness around them. "I didn't mean to frighten you. My body just seems to have made some incorrect assumptions. I wouldn't upset you for the world."

"I know that. Don't worry about it, Roger. Go to sleep."

But he was almost afraid to go to sleep, afraid of what would happen when he was unconscious. Eventually, though, holding onto a rung of the brass bed, he drifted off again out of sheer fatigue. This time when he woke he found their positions reversed, with Judy's body spooned against his, her breasts touching his shoulder blades and her left arm thrown carelessly across his waist. As before, he was aroused and conscious of the places where Judy's skin touched his. Her breathing was soft and regular against his neck. He could tell that she was asleep, and he found himself unwilling to move so much as a finger for fear of waking her and having her remove her soft body from where it pressed against him.

For long minutes he lay there, fantasizing what it would be like to roll over and kiss her. To unhook and remove her bra, to slide the panties down her legs and lose them in the covers at their feet. The thought of her naked body made his penis dance with anticipation, his throat constrict with longing. His whole body seemed to throb with need for her. And here she was pressed against him, almost as though she needed him, too.

But that was impossible. They hardly knew each other. Her body was simply responding in a way similar to his, responding to what his own body had impressed on her skin earlier. Like two longtime lovers, they shared a bed and their bodies acted like magnets to each other. He should draw away from her. He should at least awaken her. But it felt so necessary, having her there close to him, almost offering herself to him, unconsciously, graciously.

With a start she drew back from him, quickly reestablishing herself on the other side of the bed. Roger rolled over and said, "Judy? I know that didn't mean anything. It was just a reaction, like mine."

"Hell, I was hoping you hadn't noticed," she whispered.

Dim dawn light was beginning to filter its way into the room. Roger couldn't see Judy's face. Would it look stricken, or might there be evidence of contained desire? Had she been as aroused as he? Well, it didn't really matter, because neither of them had intended it. Even if the physical desire that lingered in Roger's body was matched by hers, it didn't really matter.

Suddenly, he felt achingly alone. The enormity of his betrayal of Kerri, that was not really a betrayal at all, weighed on him. His body could not possibly be aroused by another woman. Not now, not so soon at least. Someday, way in the future, he would meet someone who would remind him of her, and maybe they would get together. Probably they wouldn't. The love of his life had died—and taken all the real joy out of living. Anything he came up with now, like the laughter and stories of the previous evening, was merely a pale substitute.

As though she could sense the change in him, Judy asked, "Are you all right?"

"I'm fine." But his voice caught on the last word, and he clenched his teeth together. What a jerk he was, acting like some newly widowed man. Kerri had been dead for more than nine months now.

"Would you like me to hold you?" Judy asked hesitantly.

Angel had held him, in those early days. Comforted him, made him feel not so alone. But this wouldn't be the same thing. Judy didn't stand in the same position as Angel had. His body had never responded to Angel's presence like it did to Judy's.

When he didn't say anything, Judy added, "It would be all right, Roger. Nothing would happen. I'd be like a nurse for you, because right now you need someone to take care of you."

"Better not."

"At least let me rub your back. Roll over, and I'll see if I can't massage away some of that tension."

Reluctantly, yet willingly, he moved onto his stomach and pulled the covers down to his waist. As she ran her fingers and the palms of her hands over his back, he kept his head buried in the pillow, but he could picture her behind him in her bra. His body remained tightly wound until her hands began to circle his skin, rubbing and massaging every inch of his back. Then the sexual tension eased somewhat, and he sighed. "That's great, Judy. Want me to do yours?"

He knew before the words were out that he shouldn't have offered. But she instantly responded, "No, thanks. I'm fine."

They lay side by side in the brass bed, not touching. The soft light through the red draperies gave the room a rosy glow. Roger glanced at the watch he hadn't removed from his wrist the previous evening. Five-thirty. Way too early to get up. And he wasn't sure he could get back to sleep. Or if he did where he would wind up.

He felt Judy shift restlessly on her side of the bed.

Was it possible that she'd wanted the two of them to make love? No, or she would have let him rub her back, would have let that lead somewhere. Not that it would have. Roger would have seen to that. Wouldn't he? Hell, he hadn't felt this confused in years. His body was beginning to stir again, thinking about her.

"Are you awake?" he whispered finally.

"Yeah. I can't seem to get back to sleep."

"Maybe you could tell me now about why you left the OR for the oncology floor."

He surprised a laugh out of her, as he had several times the previous evening. Her gurgle of laughter made him smile.

"Well, it had to do with a guy I'd been going with. I met him at SF General where he was a surgery resident. We lived together for a year and a half, and when we broke up I decided to change hospitals. For a while I stayed in the OR at Fielding because that's the kind of nursing I'd been good at, but afterward I decided I wanted something different. I floated for a while, and when a permanent opening came, I grabbed it. I love the floor nursing, and I especially like oncology."

"Tell me about the surgery resident."

Judy hesitated, then said, "His name was Wayne, and he was about the best person I'd ever met. Just a really good human being, you know?"

"Sure. Like Kerri."

"Right." Her voice sounded surprised. "Like Kerri. Everyone loved him, even the prima donna surgeons. He was just so . . . nice."

"Why didn't you marry him?"

Again there was a moment's hesitation. "He never asked me. I was crazy about him, but I guess he didn't feel quite the same way about me. And then he was so *nice* about breaking up with me. He explained things, and he let me blow off steam, and he never got resentful or anything. He just didn't love me the way I loved him, and there was nothing either of us could do about that."

"I'm sorry." That seemed inadequate, and Roger added, "It wasn't that he'd fallen for someone else? Sometimes around the hospital people have these intense experiences, and they just . . . fall for each other."

"No. It might have been easier if he had." Her voice took on an uncharacteristic mocking quality. "He just didn't love *me*. There was something about me that wasn't lovable enough, I guess."

Roger rolled onto his side, a frown creasing his brow. "That's not true, and you know it. Sometimes two people weren't meant for each other. I was never so amazed as when Kerri said she loved me. Sometimes I think if she hadn't been sick, she wouldn't have."

Judy shook her head. "Of course she would have loved you, Roger. You should never doubt that."

"And you should never believe you weren't lovable enough for this Wayne to love you. He just wasn't right for you."

"Obviously not. I don't deserve to end up with such a paragon of virtue!"

"Why not?"

"Because I'm not like that." She had rolled over so that she could look at him and said earnestly, "I'm just an ordinary person, who does stupid things and loses her temper. How could someone like that be comfortable with me? I'd come home ranting about how my supervisor pissed me off, and he'd think, 'What's up with her? I know her supervisor, who's a perfectly good person.' How could he understand my bitching? How could he sympathize with it?"

Roger grinned at her. "*I'd* understand. And I bet he did, too. That's just part of life, blowing off a little steam."

Judy smiled reluctantly. "Maybe. Anyhow, that's why I left the OR. Actually, I left SF General because of him, but probably I left the Fielding OR because it was time for me to have more to do with patients than with doctors."

"Hmmm. That's an interesting way of looking at it. Something like why I want to help your nephew."

Judy murmured something indistinguishable.

"I still do, Judy. I know it seemed hard of me, acting like I was going to have Larry arrested. But it's not always a good thing to protect kids from the consequences of their actions. That's something I learned with my brother Carl. My parents kept getting him out of scrapes. It was my uncle who taught him that if he didn't like the punishment, he should forego the behavior that brought it on."

"What Larry did wasn't all that awful. Well, I mean, it was kind of understandable."

"I realize that. But, Judy, I could tell, from when I met him, that Larry wasn't just going to fall in with my plan to become my pal and let me help him. This way I have a chance of exerting some real authority."

"That doesn't mean it was fair to him."

Roger shifted onto his elbow, giving an earnest tug to the blanket so that it continued to cover him. "Sure it was. What if I'd been a stranger?"

"Then you wouldn't have let him work on your car."

"True. But I trusted him, Judy. That should have made him think twice before he took the car."

"He probably thought he'd have it back before we got home from dinner, that you'd never know."

Roger leveled an intent gaze at her. "And is that good enough for you?"

"Well, no."

"Exactly."

"But he's a teenager," she protested.

"Would you have done something like that when you were a teenager?"

Judy tsked her annoyance. "No, of course not. But

I lived in a small town where people seemed more honest and trustworthy. Kids don't always see life the way we did, Roger. They see the mean streets and the people who cheat on their taxes, the rudeness and the lack of caring all around them. They don't have the same values, even if we try to instill them. It's not as easy as it looks, damnit."

"That's what Kerri said," he admitted, frowning off at the windows. "She said you could show them by example, but if you seemed like you were from a different world, they wouldn't grasp it. But we're not in a different world than these kids, are we?"

"Their world is where their peers are. We look square and strict and confining. Larry knows kids whose parents let them stay out all night, who don't care if they do their homework, or even if they go to school."

Roger sighed. "That's really sad."

"I know it is. Even Larry knows it is. But he's come from a small town to a city, and he's confused. Too many of the kids he knows think school is a waste of time." She snorted with frustration. "Why don't kids ever hang around with the nerds who know how important an education is?"

"Hell if I know."

"What are you going to have Larry do?"

"Well, so far I've taken him to Hospital Volunteer Services to sign up, and I've assessed his knowledge of auto repair. He might actually be able to work on the car and get it running again. He seems to have some interest in that."

"Oh, right, and he can drive off in it again!"

Roger cocked his head at her. "Do you think he'd do that?"

"Honestly, I don't know. I hope not. But it's taking a chance."

"I think that's one of the best things I can do for him, Judy—take a chance on him. I hope you and Liza will let me try."

"Of course we will." Judy rolled over and added, "I'm going to try to get a little more sleep, Roger. You've worn me out."

Chapter Seven

Judy lay for some time in the twilight between waking and sleeping. Talking about Wayne, and about Larry, had indeed exhausted her. But what alarmed her was the physical arousal her body seemed unable to shake. She was perfectly aware that Roger's physical reaction had been instinctive and much against his will. She was just a female body in bed with him, to which his sleeping body had reacted in a predictable way.

For her part, she felt perfectly aware of him. She knew who he was, what his circumstances were, and still her body tingled with aroused anticipation. In the haze of near sleep she could even imagine the two of them joined, interlocked in an embrace that would have shocked him. She could picture herself seducing him. Instead of giving him a back rub to ease his tensions, she would run her hands over his body in an entirely provocative way, hoping for his arousal, willing it, stimulating it. She would be the aggressor, he the passive object of her desire.

Sleep still eluded her. Judy rolled over onto her stomach, hoping the hardness of the mattress would dull the ache in her body. Roger's proximity was tantalizing, making erotic daydreams shimmer through her mind. She felt the echo of his hardness between her legs and wondered what would have happened if she had eased herself onto him. Would he have responded automatically, too sleep-numbed to realize who she was? Would his hands have circled her, nudging the bra away so they could touch the waiting skin of her breasts?

Cut it out! she admonished herself. Count to a hundred, slowly. Think of nothing else. Let your body relax. It's just a little arousal. Big deal. It happens to people all the time. One, two, three, four . . .

When she awoke she found herself alone in the bed. Roger and his clothes were both missing. She reached over for her watch on the bedside table and found that it was seven-thirty, still earlier than breakfast would be served in the dining room. After a few minutes of just lying there speculating on where he might be, Judy climbed out of bed and went to the window. Sure enough, he was standing down by the river, staring past the bridge with a faraway expression on his face.

He wouldn't want her to join him. He was probably thinking about Kerri and wishing she was there with him. He would be castigating himself for the trick his body had played on him during the night, and hoping Judy wouldn't be upset by his actions. He was thinking about how to apologize in a tactful way for his body's unconscious treachery. And wishing he'd never accepted her invitation to play miniature golf.

Judy could read it all in his face. She was good at reading faces. Except that she'd learned, with OR patients, that she read a great deal more into them than was necessarily there. She had a habit of projecting her own thoughts or wishes or expectations onto them, when there was no information forthcoming. Well, she was sure she wasn't wrong about Roger. What else could he be thinking?

With a sigh she dropped the red curtain back in place. It was a good thing he wasn't here, a good thing she had fallen asleep when she had, rather than acting on her impulse to try to seduce him. Or was that just a dream she'd had? Judy shook her head in mock despair and pulled her shirt on. The whole thing had been blown out of proportion in her mind. She and Roger were just friends stuck here overnight. Period. Everything else was lurid imaginings, the natural sequelae to two (almost) naked bodies sharing a bed.

Judy drew on her white pants and fluffed her hair with her fingers. A glance in the mirror assured her that no man in his right mind would be interested in coupling with this sleepy-eyed, wiry-haired sprite. But lurking at the back of her eyes was a spark that hadn't been there the previous evening. Judy turned away from the mirror with a groan.

Downstairs the coffee was set out on a cart. The dining room was wood-beamed and cozy, but the doors to the patio overlooking the river stood temptingly open. Judy filled a cup with coffee and wandered out onto the patio. No one else was around, including Roger. She sipped slowly at the coffee, trying not to think of anything at all except the sun gleaming off the river and the bits of mist still rising from the water farther downstream.

In a while she relaxed, soothed by the peaceful scene. The redwoods stood timeless and tall, the river quietly flowing below them. Her mind drifted to the hospital where she had spent such a harried week. Things began to fall in place now, with the chance to look back on them. The deaths, merciful in many ways. Some forms of cancer were more devastating than others, causing more pain and suffering. With the patient's help, they were learning to rate the pain, and to give appropriate dosages of medications to alleviate it. She had taken a continuing education class in pain management, taught by an anesthesiologist.

Which reminded her of a question that had popped into her mind during the week, one which Roger could no doubt answer. And, as if in summons to her thought, he appeared out on the terrace holding a cup of coffee. He came directly to her, with a smile. "Glorious day," he said, allowing his body to drop easily onto the chair opposite her. "They'll bring our fruit and rolls out in a minute, and take our order for eggs or pancakes."

"There wasn't anyone around when I came down."

"I think breakfast starts at eight on Sundays. We aren't in any hurry, are we?"

He seemed perfectly relaxed. The anxiety Judy had expected him to carry over from their physical contact during the night did not seem to remain, which surprised her. His guilt about being turned on had been very apparent at the time. What had he said to himself to lessen that guilt?

Probably that he knew very well he wasn't attracted to her, in the ordinary course of things. That it was just the bizarre situation in which they found themselves that had tripped a very natural instinct in him. And that it wouldn't happen again.

Judy sighed and asked him whether he recommended Patient Controlled Analgesia machines or a spinal block to patients for pain medication after surgery. He happily settled into explaining that his preference was very seldom the patient's, and took his time giving her his reasoning on the subject. Before she even noticed time passing, a plate of steaming pancakes was set in front of each of them and she realized that she was starving.

As she poured syrup over her stack, she asked Roger, "What are you planning to do with Larry? A hundred and fifty hours is a long time."

"Too long, do you think?" he asked, squinting against the sun.

"Probably."

"He doesn't have anything else to do this summer, does he?"

"No, but that doesn't mean he should provide you with free labor, either."

"Well, only a little of it's for me, actually," he replied, undisturbed. "We've signed him up for volunteering in the emergency department. I had to pull a few strings for that, but Steve helped me, and it's one of the most interesting places. He'll get to see what's going on, and run samples to the lab, and stock the cabinets."

"He's not interested in medicine, Roger."

"How do you know?"

"Well, I'm his aunt and I'm a nurse, and he's never asked me one question about the hospital."

Roger waved this aside with an airy gesture. "They've got to see blood before they're really grabbed. Something dramatic. Fielding gets enough trauma cases that he's going to see some of the real stuff."

Judy wrinkled her nose. "Spoken like a man. Couldn't someone get interested in medicine just because they wanted to heal the sick and help the disabled?"

"Nope. It's got to be epic to get through to someone like Larry. One day they'll bring in a gunshot wound bleeding out, and Larry will watch them save him. That should do it."

"Not if he's not meant for medicine."

"Well, maybe not," he agreed as he set down his fork and picked up the syrup pitcher again. "I'm also going to have him work on my car. Just in case a more mechanical, brain-saving career seems to be what interests him. After all, he was the one who thought he could fix it the other day."

"From rattling. Not putting it back together again!"

"Still. He took some kind of auto shop class, Judy. I suppose he agreed to it because he didn't want to have to study too hard, but he probably learned something. Let's see if he can put it to good use."

"What if he takes your car again?"

Roger looked very serious. "I'd report him to the police again, Judy, and this time I'd make sure he went through the juvenile court system. I've told him that. It won't do him the least bit of good to think he can get away with this kind of thing." He sat back and regarded her curiously. "Do you think I'm being too hard on him?"

Embarrassed, she shrugged. "Yes, but I know I shouldn't. He needs to learn to take responsibility, and he needs to have someone insist that he involve himself in something useful. I just sort of feel like maybe it's taking advantage of him to make him do work that you'd pay someone else to do. I mean, that's not really community service."

"Ah, I see. Like he should be scrubbing graffiti off building walls or streetcars, huh? Hell, Judy, I think he'd rather work on the car."

"Probably he would. Still."

"Juvenile court would have put him in the hands of someone who could arrange for service like that, Judy. I can't. Getting him to volunteer at Fielding is as close as I can come, and they're not equipped to have him put in all those hours."

"I know."

"Besides, I think we're going to *teach* him something this way, not just make him work off the hours. I had him get a book on car repair and part of his assignment is to read up on what the Audi needs." He grinned at her. "Maybe we could have him read up on the Civic for you."

That drew a reluctant smile from her. "If it hadn't been for his taking my spare tire and not replacing it, my car would have gotten us back to San Francisco last night."

"And we wouldn't be sitting here enjoying the sun and the redwoods and the river."

Nor would we have slept in the same bed last night and gotten all confused sexually, she added in her own mind. Aloud she added, "To say nothing of the pancakes."

"Yeah, they're good." His gaze wandered to the river where he stared unseeing for a few minutes. After a while he blinked his eyes and turned back to her. "His computer skills aren't very good, either. I think we should do something about that."

"Don't look at me. I'm just learning myself." She took a sip of her orange juice. "How have you managed to find out all this in such a short time, Roger? He hardly talks to us at all."

"I asked him. Kerri used to tell me that adults didn't talk enough to kids, to find out what they were really thinking. Teenagers just blow you off when you first approach them, she said. You have to be kind of specific."

"In what way?" Judy asked, feeling a little defensive. Hadn't she and Liza tried hard to get Larry to open up?

"Like about the car repair, instead of saying, 'What have you learned in shop so far?' I asked Larry if they'd worked on welding or electric systems or the engine or the spark plugs. And I did it while we had the Audi's hood open, so we could discuss what was going on there. He's interested in cars, but I suspect it's just because he likes driving them and not because he envisions a career in car repair. But you never know."

"He seems smart enough to go to college, but his grades are abysmal. And he's not likely to go if he doesn't have some goal."

Roger nodded. "That's exactly why I think it will help if I work with him. To help him develop some kind of ambition. It could be medicine, it could be cars, it could be computers, it could be business. Don't they have career counseling at his school?"

"Sure, but he hasn't been interested."

"I'll get him interested," Roger promised with surprising confidence.

With just the slightest edge to her voice, Judy said, "I'll bet you will."

"You're still a little annoyed with me, but don't worry. Everything will work out okay."

"Pollyanna."

"Hardly. But I do have a hunch about this. Larry's basically a good kid."

Judy nodded. "I think he is. But we haven't had any luck getting him to take responsibility at home. He just blows us off when we try to get him to do housework."

"Maybe you and Liza are going to have to set down some rules of your own for him."

"And if he doesn't obey them?"

"Then he doesn't get certain things."

"Such as what?"

"His meals prepared for him. His laundry done." He tilted his head questioningly at her rueful expression. "What?"

"So he'll go to school in dirty clothes. And make a mess of the kitchen fixing his own food. We've tried that."

"Judy, you don't allow him to get away with it. You start cutting back on other privileges—like watching television, driving the car. You might even have to ground him."

"I'm not his mother, and Liza can't do it consistently."

"Sure she can. You just keep insisting that she do it. Tell her it's for her son's own good."

"Larry hates that kind of talk."

"So what?" Roger sighed. "I know I'm making it sound easier than it is. But what could be more important than impressing the right kind of values on the kid?"

"I know, I know. We'll work on it. Maybe it's all to the good that you've been given a little authority over Larry, that he *has* to listen to you."

"Yeah, that's what I thought." Roger grinned broadly. "I figure I wouldn't have gotten anywhere the way I first planned it."

His smile positively transformed his face. At that moment he looked lighthearted and charming and accessible. Judy felt a sharp desire to touch him, to put her hand on his cheek in a loving, possessive way. She wished mightily that they were here as a couple. The thought of making him happy was irresistible. Yesterday it had been a gesture of friendship; today it felt more like a personal need.

She wanted to spend time with him because there was something about him that attracted her. Was it just the nursing streak in her—wanting to make him feel better? Wanting to see him heal from the devastating wound he'd received? Judy wasn't sure. It didn't feel like that, sitting here opposite him. And it hadn't felt like that in bed this morning. But maybe that was different. It had been a long time since she'd had a sexual partner.

Roger had gone on to talk about the teenage sons of friends of his. Judy listened with only part of her attention, though her gaze remained locked on his animated face. His curly brown hair, which still looked damp, caught the gleam of the morning sun. His brown eyes spoke as eloquently as his gesticulating hands. He was there to please her, too, in his way. Judy could tell he wanted to win her over about Larry. There was nothing more personal about his attempts to amuse and cajole her. Too bad.

Accepting the situation for what it was, she settled back in her chair and brought her full attention to bear on him. If there wasn't any more personal connection between them, at least there was the link of Larry. Judy wondered if Roger might not be on the right track with her nephew, and she was determined to learn what she could from his methods.

By the time they finished breakfast the Triple A service truck had arrived. The driver towed Judy's Civic to the nearest service station, in Guerneville, with Judy and Roger seated beside him on the slippery bench seat of his truck. Roger noted Judy's profound relief when she was able to have the tire fixed right there and her satisfaction when her car was once again restored to functioning. He had thought perhaps they'd spend the day at the river, maybe wading in the shallow water near the shore, or playing another game of miniature golf, but Judy looked determined to get him home as soon as possible.

"I've kept you away far too long," she apologized as she rolled down her window to let in a hot breeze. "You probably had a thousand things planned for the weekend."

"Nope. Hardly anything. I was going to go over to Cliff and Angel's for dinner tonight." He glanced at his watch. It was only ten-fifteen. "And obviously I still can. Do you want to come?"

Judy looked shocked. "No, of course not. I wasn't invited. They hardly know me. You can't just bring an extra person along."

"Sure I could. They wouldn't mind."

"Well, thanks, but no, thanks. I have . . . other stuff I have to do."

It seemed to Roger that he had embarrassed her, or made her uncomfortable in some way. She kept her gaze on the road as she headed the car back toward Route 101. Probably, he thought, she was remembering how badly he had behaved last night. Undoubtedly, she wanted to dump him at his house as soon as possible. He had decided as he wandered by the river that morning that it was best to ignore the episode, but who could blame her for not forgetting?

"Maybe we could do something together with Larry," he suggested after a while. "See a ball game, or go for a picnic in the park."

"Larry would just want to subtract the time from the hours he owes you, Roger, and that would hurt your feelings."

"No, it wouldn't. Well, maybe it would, but I could choose something with a point to it, like going to the Exploratorium or the Lawrence Livermore exhibit."

"No, I think we should keep your dealings with Larry separate. Then he's more likely to continue to respect your authority."

It seemed to Roger that she was being deliberately discouraging of their being better friends. Maybe even that she was annoyed with him because of what he was trying to do. Roger wasn't used to trying to figure out what women really meant. Angel was very blunt with him, and Nan had pretty much followed her example. Roger knew for a fact that Judy was ordinarily a blunt sort of woman who spoke her mind. So why was she acting this way?

When they came out of the redwood-forested area of the River Road and began driving alongside vine-covered fields, Roger sighed inwardly and decided he was to blame for Judy's silence. Naturally, she was too polite to indicate her disapproval of his behavior last night, when it was because of her car's problems that they had had to stay together. She didn't want to spend any time with him, fearing that he'd come on to her in some way. Probably, she thought his inviting her to Angel and Cliff's was all a part of this scenario, and his suggestion that she join him in spending time with Larry.

Well, she was right to keep her distance from him. He obviously couldn't be trusted to behave himself, when he was acting on purely animal instinct. But he wasn't always acting on instinct. He was a civilized human being, and for the most part his behavior could be trusted to exhibit that fact.

So Roger set himself to win Judy over with hospital stories and glimpses of his youthful peccadilloes, and soon he had her laughing and answering questions about herself that she had seemed reluctant earlier to consider.

And then they were back in San Francisco, and she was depositing him at his house. Roger asked if she would come in for lunch, but she said, "Thanks, but I'd better get home. I didn't intend to spend the night away, and I have a lot to catch up on. Thanks for being such a good sport, Roger."

"Thanks for putting up with me."

He watched as she backed the Civic out of his driveway and drove away. Funny. It left him feeling a little bereft. Even remembering that he was going to Angel and Cliff's for dinner didn't quite lift his spirits to where they had been on the ride home.

And he realized he hadn't thought of Kerri for the last several hours.

Chapter Eight

By Monday Judy had developed a personal mantra that went something like: "Roger Janek is a friend and Larry's mentor." Whenever her thoughts drifted off to any aspect of the weekend, most especially the incidents in bed together, she would repeat her mantra and firmly turn her thoughts to something else. Monday was often a busy day, catching up on patient tests and admissions that had slowed over the weekend. Judy found herself exhausted when she had given report to the nurse taking over. All she wanted to do was disappear from the building.

As she hurried down the corridor to the elevators, she realized that the boy coming toward her was her nephew Larry. He had never come to see her before, and for a moment she felt a stab of panic. What now? But she could see that he was grinning from ear to ear, and her heartbeat slowed accordingly.

"You'll never guess what, Judy!" he exclaimed. "There was this paramedic crew bringing in a guy from a car wreck, and they had him in MAST pants and all, because he'd been bleeding. God, there was blood everywhere. And they let me hold the IV bag while we ran him into the emergency room because everyone else was helping with a guy in cardiac arrest. It was awesome!"

Clever Roger. He had known just where Larry would find the most excitement. No patient book cart for a kid who was into cars. Put him where things were happening.

Judy punched the elevator button. "Sounds like you're getting to see the real thing. Did they save him?"

"They stabilized him for surgery," Larry said, undoubtedly quoting some emergency-room personnel. "But they sent me out as soon as they had enough people to help," he admitted grudgingly. Then his face lit again. "But I went outside with the paramedics, and they were still talking about the case. They were just drinking coffee when they got the call. Speed City. You can't waste any time when it's an injury accident."

Judy let him babble on, remembering the excitement of her first encounters with emergency medicine. It was heartwarming to see Larry so caught up in something besides his own problems, or cars. Hadn't the drama of surgery drawn her to the operating room? Maybe this experience would give Larry some ideas about going into medicine.

"How old do you have to be to be a paramedic?" he asked.

"I don't know, exactly. People are emergency medical technicians, EMTs, first. And I suppose they can start doing that when they're eighteen."

"God, a year and a half. That's a long time." His brows drew down over his brown eyes. "Maybe they have junior ones or something."

"You could ask around."

"Would you do that for me?"

"Why wouldn't you do it yourself?"

He shrugged. "I don't know any of the people here yet. They'd help you find out, wouldn't they?"

"I'm not sure hospital people necessarily know a lot about EMTs or paramedics, Larry. Your school guidance counselor would probably be more helpful."

He wrinkled his nose. "Missi leman? He doesn't know anything."

"Bet he does." Judy, exhausted, jockeyed her nephew into the elevator that had finally arrived. "But it will be too long until school starts again, so check it out at a library, or ask Roger."

"EMTs? I haven't the slightest," Roger said. "I know they have to have a fair amount of training—CPR and stuff like that. Did you ask at a library?"

"They've cut back on their hours, and I had to get here on time."

Roger could see that Larry was frustrated and irritable. At Roger's request, he had come to the house in Laurel Heights at five-thirty, but Roger had been delayed for half an hour and had no means of communicating with Larry. Even before this incident, Roger had assured Larry that if he had to wait, that would count as part of his time, but the boy obviously felt abused by having to cool his heels on the entry porch with nothing to do. Roger could have pointed out that it would have been a good time to start on his reading about the Audi, but he felt the strategy would merely antagonize his youthful visitor.

He unlocked and pushed open the door, gesturing for Larry to precede him. "What's got you interested in EMTs?"

Larry regained some of his equanimity by explaining what had happened to him the previous day at the hospital. Roger thought ruefully that it would be just like the boy to find the sirens and trauma of the paramedic world more exciting than the more subtle rewards of hospital medicine, even in the emergency room.

It was Tuesday, and his housekeeper came in that day. The house looked great, as always, and he could smell the meal she'd left warming in the oven. Larry had been invited for a working dinner, and Roger was shifting mental gears about what work they were going to do. Nothing like the information highway to intrigue a teenager—if they could find something about EMTs. And they probably could.

Roger had Larry help him set the table while he brought in the chicken casserole. There was a green salad in the refrigerator that he anointed with ranch dressing after getting Larry's agreement. Once, soon after he returned to his house, he had had Cliff and Angel to dinner, but having Larry was different. Roger couldn't treat him exactly as a guest, since he wanted the boy to learn how to take part in a family dinner the way Roger had as a kid—setting the table, cleaning up afterward, helping with the dishes. All things that apparently Larry wasn't accomplishing at home.

Roger talked to him while they worked, asking him about his emergency-room experience with the paramedics. When they sat down to eat, he gave Larry a broader knowledge of what a paramedic did at the scene of an automobile accident, a near drowning, an unscheduled childbirth, a poisoning, or for a gunshot wound. He told stories that he knew would capture Larry's attention, all the while wondering if shooting for paramedic was as high as Larry's sights should be raised. Not everyone, he reminded himself, was interested in becoming a doctor.

"Do you ever talk with your aunt about her work?" he asked.

"Nah. She's just a nurse."

Roger shook his head in bemusement. "Just a nurse, huh? Is there something wrong with that?"

"Well, hey, it's not as if she was a doctor or something. She just empties bedpans and stuff like that."

"How do you know that's all she does if you haven't talked with her?"

Larry shrugged off the question. "Everyone knows what nurses do. They follow doctors' orders."

"And you don't think paramedics do?"

That brought Larry up short. "Well, they're on their own out there, aren't they? No doctor rides along with them."

"True, but they can't give certain treatments without a doctor's say-so. They get specially trained so they can give CPR and assess a situation, but it still comes down to a doctor's decision about how to keep the patient alive until they reach the hospital."

Larry, quicker than Roger had anticipated, cocked his head and said, "You think I should want to become a doctor, don't you?"

"Not really. I think the point I was trying to make," he admitted, "was that your aunt would probably have a lot to tell you about medicine that would fascinate you. She worked in an operating room for a number of years, and now she works with oncology patients who call on the internal strength of their caregivers. You need a certain kind of strength to be a paramedic, too, Larry. You run into a lot of desperate, frightened people in emergencies. What you say to them, and how you treat them, can be every bit as important as what you do for them."

"That's just a moral," Larry scoffed. "Grown-ups are always trying to impress morals on kids. Every other television sitcom has a moral. Life's not like that."

Roger found the boy's cynicism more amusing than offensive. "That depends on how you look at it. Life doesn't happen in half-hour chunks, but it's certainly fraught with moral dilemmas. How are you going to know how to respond to them if you don't have guidance? Do you think you're born with some kind of moral fiber?"

"Yeah, I guess I do." Larry forked a bite of salad into his mouth and chewed on it thoughtfully. "I can make up my own mind about that kind of stuff."

"Okay, let's take a situation and work through it." Roger, intent on making a point, had abandoned his food, though he sipped occasionally at a glass of Riesling. "Let's take the night you drove off in my car, shall we?"

Larry moaned. "Oh, great. Now we're really going to have a moral lesson."

"Maybe. But listen, I just want to understand where you're coming from, okay?"

Larry looked ceilingward. "You forgot to add 'dude.' "

"Don't be a wiseass. People of my generation used

the phrase 'where you're coming from' before you were born."

"Sure. Right."

"So on the night I came over to take Liza and Judy out to dinner, explain to me what was going on in your mind. Why did you offer to fix the car? Were you already thinking about driving off with it?"

"Mmmm, no. I just like messing around with cars. And it seemed like I could do something to make yours not rattle, that it wouldn't be hard."

"But why would you want to do that?" Roger pressed. "I was a stranger to you."

Larry lifted his shoulders. "Hey, I just did. It was an Audi. The cars we work on in school are usually cheap junkers. I liked the idea of putzing around on an Audi, even though it looked like sh— dirt."

"And what did you think about me?"

"Nothing. You were just a guy. Mom had said you were a doctor, but you didn't look snooty or anything."

"How about money? Did you think I'd give you money for doing the work?"

Larry flushed slightly and looked out the window into the garden. "Maybe. You know, being a doctor and everything, it seemed like you might slip me something. Everyone knows doctors have lots of money to throw around."

Roger grinned. "Did your aunt tell you that?"

"Hell, no! Judy thinks doctors are really tight-fisted."

Roger wondered briefly where that had come from, but he ignored it for the moment. "It's just general knowledge, then. So part of your reason for wanting to fix the car was that I'd pay you for doing it."

"I guess."

"Did it matter to you if you did a good job of it?"

Larry regarded him with suspicion. "What do you mean? Like I'd cheat you?"

"No, Larry, I'm trying to figure out if along with your enjoyment of doing certain kinds of things you have a drive to do them well. Or is just getting them done as fast as possible the main criteria?"

"I work fast," the boy said. "I knew I could have it done before you got back."

Roger couldn't be sure whether he was evading the question or simply didn't understand the concept of quality. "When did you decide to include your friend?"

"I always borrow tools from him. We don't have many because my mom and my aunt aren't that interested in working on their cars. Mike's dad works at a garage, and I think he lifts their tools from time to time, so he's got quite a collection."

Oh, great, Roger thought. Now I'm going to become a party to grand larceny. "I suppose that doesn't bother anyone, his dad stealing tools?"

"They don't pay him what he's worth, so he slips something out of there every once in a while. Everybody does it."

"No, everybody doesn't do it," Roger insisted. "That's just a weak excuse, a poor justification for doing what you want to do. Everybody doesn't cheat on their taxes, either, in case you've heard that, too."

Larry just stared at him, looking superior. Roger sighed. Where did these attitudes get started? He would have sworn Judy and her sister didn't promote them with the teenager. So who did? Were Larry's contemporaries all this disillusioned and potentially dishonest? Well, Roger refused to get distracted by that issue. He had other matters to track down. He could tackle that one later.

"So you went to your friend Mike's and got the necessary tools. What did you tell Mike about what you were doing?"

Larry looked sullen. "I just told him I was fixing an Audi. He said he'd help."

"But if he helped, you'd have to share any money with him, wouldn't you?"

"I suppose."

"But that didn't matter."

Looking uncomfortable, Larry shifted in his chair. "I didn't know if I was going to get any."

"I see. So the two of you worked on the car and then decided to drive it." Roger frowned slightly at the glass of wine he held in his right hand. "Did you tell him you weren't supposed to take it off the block?"

"No."

"Why not?"

"I just didn't." Larry had taken to knocking his foot against the center post of the dining table. At a gesture from Roger he stopped, but his knee continued to swing rhythmically back and forth. He had stopped eating his meal, though there was still a piece of chicken on his plate.

"Well, think about it," Roger instructed. "Was it your decision to drive the car off the block? Did you want to impress Mike in some way? Or maybe it would have been embarrassing to admit that you weren't supposed to leave the block. Was it any of those things?"

"I don't know. We just did it. It's kind of babyish to have to drive just on one block. You have to turn around in people's driveways, and it didn't really give us a good idea of whether or not the car was still rattling."

"What I'm getting at, Larry, is whether you felt any pressure from outside you to do something you weren't supposed to do."

"What difference does it make? We thought we'd be back before you got home."

"So if you could fool me, that made everything okay?"

Larry pushed his chair away from the table. "This

is stupid. I don't want to talk about it anymore. We've been over it and over it. I don't see what good it does."

In fact, the two of them hadn't discussed Larry's taking the Audi for a joyride since the night it had happened. Roger could feel that his frustration had reached an almost intolerable level, however, and he decided to back off. "Okay, we'll drop it for now. But we'll talk about it again, Larry, and I hope in the meantime you'll think about what motivated you."

"Oh, sure."

The boy's sarcasm wasn't lost on him, but Roger felt there was a point of diminishing returns here. And he still had one goal to accomplish. "Okay, so before we sit down to the computer, I want you to help with the dishes."

Larry's shoulders set stubbornly, and he remained seated in his chair.

Roger suppressed a sigh. "We'll do them together, but we're not going to search for EMT information on the computer until they're done."

Larry glared at him, pushed his chair back, and stomped into the kitchen. And I asked for this, Roger thought wonderingly.

When Larry had left, Roger pulled the phone on his desk closer and dialed Jerry Stoner's number. The psychiatrist answered almost immediately. "Maybe this wasn't such a great idea," Roger burst out without preamble. "What do I know about teenagers?"

"As much as anyone, probably," Jerry said. "You've been one. Tell me how it's going."

For twenty minutes Roger poured out the story of his encounters with the sullen youngster. The last thing he expected to hear was Jerry saying, "I'm impressed. You're actually making progress with him, Roger. You've got to expect him to press the limits every time he can. That's what kids do."

"So I'm not really screwing this up?"

"Hell, no. Look where you've gotten. The kid has a real interest in the future for the first time, and you're going to be able to help him find ways to work toward it. You got him to help with the dishes to further that aim. Next time maybe he'll do it because you provided dinner and it's the appropriate thing to do. Hey, you've got a real toehold, Roger."

Roger laughed. "You could have fooled me, but I'll take your word for it, Jerry. You're the shrink."

"Take my word that you're sounding better every day, too," Jerry said. "I'm really pleased for you, Roger."

Surprised, Roger could only say, "Well, thanks."

"Just remember that today's teenagers almost all have a rough time. Keep up your good work with the kid. It's obviously helping both of you."

As he put down the receiver, Roger realized that it

was true he was feeling better all the time. But he wasn't sure Larry had everything to do with it.

Though there was a separate section in the Fielding cafeteria for the doctors, they didn't always sit in it. Still, Judy was startled to look up and find that it was Angel Crawford who hovered over the table, seeking permission to join her. "Sure. Have a seat." Judy shifted her tray so that Angel could set hers down. "The fajitas are good. I think you'll like them."

Angel wearily lowered her pregnant body into the comfortable seat opposite Judy and smiled. "This being pregnant during your residency is a bit much. Of course, I chose it, so I shouldn't complain."

"Hey, complain all you want. Probably no one around here listens to you anyway."

"How true." Angel regarded the fajitas with skepticism. "Are they pretty spicy? I haven't been doing very well with spicy food lately."

Judy finished chewing a bite and gestured to the peppers. "Skip those and you'll probably be okay."

Angel nodded, and for a while the two women ate their meals in silence. "Not bad," Angel agreed. "I don't suppose the cafeteria at the hospital in Wisconsin is going to serve fajitas."

"Probably not."

"Still, I'm hoping Cliff will like it there. Being a big fish in a little pond is a whole lot more exciting than being a big fish in a huge pond."

Judy wasn't sure where this was leading, but she casually agreed that Dr. Lenzini might find his new situation rewarding. She was aware, as most of the people at Fielding were, that Cliff had agreed to live in Wisconsin because Angel wanted to return there. Somehow, she suspected, it was his way of proving that he was capable of compromise.

"Roger was over for dinner the other night," Angel said.

"Yes, he said he was going."

"It sounds like he's gotten involved with your nephew in a slightly different way than he'd expected."

"Well, Larry's problems were what piqued Roger's interest in the first place. Poor man, he had no idea what he was letting himself in for. Which is not necessarily a bad thing," Judy mused. "We're actually seeing some signs of change in Larry. Just little things. He put his clothes in the laundry basket yesterday instead of leaving them on the floor of his room. Maybe Roger's a good influence."

"I wouldn't be surprised." Angel pushed a pepper off the flour tortilla on her plate and cut another bite of fajita. "Roger thought you and your sister might not have understood why he went along with the policeman about the community service hours."

Judy shrugged. "At the time we didn't. But it was certainly better than having to go to juvenile court with Larry. And then Roger explained it the other day, so we're okay with it."

Again the two women were silent as they continued to eat, but Judy sensed that Angel hadn't come to discuss pregnancy, or Wisconsin, or Larry. She suspected Angel was struggling to approach her subject in just the right way—one which wouldn't upset Judy or make her feel as if Angel were interfering. But Angel was a remarkably no-nonsense woman, so her next comments were no real surprise to Judy.

"I wanted," she finally said, meeting Judy's gaze with her gray-green eyes, "to talk with you about Roger. And you."

"There is no Roger and me," Judy rushed to assure her. "We just got stuck in the Russian River because my car had a flat."

"Did you?" Angel laughed. "He didn't tell us that. He did say he'd invited you to come with him to dinner on Sunday. That would have been fine, Judy. We'd have loved having you."

"Thanks, but it seemed an imposition. And we got back really early in the day."

"Heaven forbid that you should have to spend the whole day together," Angel murmured.

Judy's face flushed slightly, but she said nothing.

"Roger's a really special person," Angel continued. "And he's had a very difficult time this last year. In some ways he feels his life is over, but of course it's not. He's a loving, generous man, and he's not going to be closed down forever because of Kerri's death. It may take a little more time, though, before he can see that. I wouldn't want you to get discouraged with him . . . if, you know, you thought he was someone special."

Angel was peering at her intently, but Judy didn't know what to say. She was spared the necessity when another arrival at the table distracted both of them. Angel's husband, Cliff Lenzini, was a man of six-four or six-five, with unruly black hair and demanding brown eyes. He was in his mid-thirties and a well-respected surgeon at Fielding.

His wife made room for his tray. "Cliff! You remember Judy Povalski don't you?"

"Who else could it possibly be?" he muttered. "Didn't Roger mention her on Sunday?"

"He's feeling a little cranky today," Angel explained with a patience belied by her grin. "He was going to talk with you yesterday, but he couldn't find you."

"I was not," Cliff insisted. On his plate were two fajitas and an incongruous corn muffin. He kicked his chair into submission and sat down. "I just wanted to make sure we were all talking about the same Judy. Oncology floor, right?"

"Right." Judy's gaze shifted back and forth between the two of them. "So you were all talking about me on Sunday. I guess I might as well have come with Roger. You know, I'm very well aware that he's still grieving for Kerri. I don't have my sights on him or anything."

"You should," Cliff retorted. He had already taken a bite of the fajita and paused a moment to chew it. "He's been moping around for almost a year. He needs someone to bring him out of it, and Angel and I are going to be out of here in a few weeks. It's really stupid of him to have taken on your nephew, but you just can't talk to him when his mind's made up."

"You'd have talked him out of marrying Kerri if you'd had your way," Angel reminded him.

"Well, she was dying," he said bluntly. "People just don't go around marrying dying people. At least no one I ever knew."

"Well, now you know one." Angel turned to Judy. "Cliff's trying hard to be patient with Roger, but patience doesn't come naturally to Cliff."

"It does, too," he protested, though not very convincingly. "But, hell, it's time for Roger to get on with things. You're a good woman, Judy. We just wanted you to know that we like the idea of you and Roger, you know, becoming friends and all."

"He's so tactful." Angel squeezed her spouse's hand. "Don't you just love him?"

Wisely, Judy neglected to answer what was, after all, a rhetorical question. "I'm afraid the two of you have gotten the wrong idea. Roger's not interested in me."

"Well, maybe not yet," Cliff agreed. "But he could be, and we'd be really pleased if he were."

"Thanks. I appreciate your vote of confidence. But Roger and I are just friends. He's trying to get my nephew turned around, and my sister and I are grateful. I don't think you can expect anything more than that to come of it."

Angel nodded her understanding. "We're giving ourselves a farewell party just before we leave. I hope you'll come."

Judy rose and picked up her tray. "Thanks. That would be fun. Sorry, but I've got to get back to the floor."

As she put her tray on the revolving rack, she glanced back at the two of them and saw that they were still watching her. Certainly, they made a handsome couple. But where had they gotten the idea that Roger might be interested in her? Not from him, she'd be willing to bet. With a quick wave of her hand, Judy hurried out into the corridor and up the stairs to the sixth floor.

Chapter Nine

Judy received an invitation in the mail to the farewell party Angel and Cliff were giving for themselves. She was aware that there had been several occasions given by their various departments or friends, but this was, quite logically, the only event in which she had been included. Because she didn't know either of them very well, she was considering simply skipping the party and thanking Angel after the fact for the invitation.

The party, scheduled for two days after Angel finished her residency, was being squeezed in between that date and the one a week later when the couple would be departing, permanently, for Wisconsin. Most people at Fielding predicted that they would be back, that Cliff would never last in the wilds of Wisconsin, that Angel would be drawn back by San Francisco's charm—and the fact that Cliff was holding onto the house he had owned for so long on Twin Peaks.

Liza had taken to urging Judy to go, right up until the night of the party. "Look, you don't have to work tonight. They invited you in person. What more could you want?" she asked.

Judy had her back turned to her sister as she wrote out a check for the gas and electricity. "They only did it because they think I'm interested in Roger."

"Are you?"

"I don't know."

Liza sounded surprised. "What do you mean, you don't know? You mean you might be?"

At the time, Judy had said very little about her time at the Russian River with Roger. Other than passing on the information about Roger's intentions with regard to helping Larry, it had seemed easiest to let her sister think of the episode as a nonevent. Besides, Judy didn't *want* to be interested in Roger. Knowing his situation, that would be stupid.

Judy slipped the check into an envelope and shrugged. "He's a nice guy, Liza. And I find him kind of attractive."

"Roger?" Liza asked incredulously. "Sure, he's cute enough, but he tugs at his ears. Wouldn't that drive you nuts?"

"I can't say it's bothered me yet. In fact, I find it rather endearing."

"Wow." Liza regarded her keenly. "When did this happen?"

"Nothing's *happened,* Liza. It's just that, if everything were equal, I might be interested in Roger. I don't know that I would, but it's a possibility."

"Well, it's more than a possibility that I'm interested in Phil," her sister admitted with a flush. "He's taken me out to lunch twice and to the movies once, but maybe that's just because we work together. He's so handsome, and so smart, and so *everything,* that I can't imagine why he'd be interested in me."

"Of course he'd be interested in you, silly. You're charming and pretty and loving. What more could a man want?"

"Lots. I've never even gone to college, and he's a lawyer. So I have to be careful not to, you know, just sort of fall for him. He may only be passing the time until someone really right for him comes along."

"I doubt it, but time will tell. You've said for a long time how nice he is to you at the office."

Liza sighed. "I suppose I shouldn't be dating a guy from my office, but he's just so *terrific.* How could I resist?"

The phone rang, and Judy lifted the receiver from the wall. "Hello."

"Judy? It's Roger."

"Hi, Roger," she said, winking at her sister. "Larry's not in right now. Want me to take a message?"

"No, I wanted to talk to you. Angel said you're

coming tonight and suggested I give you a ride because there will be a lot of cars, and parking could get tricky."

"I haven't actually decided whether I'm coming."

"But you've got to come! It's their farewell party."

Judy laughed. "I don't know them the way you do, Roger. Of course you should go."

"Why wouldn't you come?"

"I've had a hard day. I'm exhausted."

"But you aren't going to have to do anything. I'd pick you up and deposit you right in front of their door. You could just relax and enjoy the party. And they always have great food. Angel gets it catered."

"Smart woman. But I've already eaten, and I thought I'd just plop down in front of the television or pick up a good book."

"Don't you like partying with people from Fielding?" he asked, sounding more curious than reproachful.

"To be honest, it's not always easy for me to talk with people I don't know very well, Roger. And I won't know most of the people there."

"But you'll have a lot in common with them. They'd love to hear your stories about the gypsies and the leeches."

"Well . . ."

"Judy," he said earnestly, "this is going to be my first real Fielding party since Kerri died. I don't want to disappoint Angel and Cliff, so I'll go no matter what, but it would make it easier for me if you'd come with me."

Judy wasn't sure she wanted to be his safety net, but she found herself saying, "All right, Roger, but I probably won't want to stay late."

"Thanks, Judy. Pick you up at eight."

Liza grinned at her as she hung up the phone. "I'm glad he talked you into it. Bet you have a great time."

"Humph." Judy regarded her sister suspiciously. "Are you expecting Phil here this evening?"

Liza blushed. "Yes. And I'd introduce him to you, Judy, except that I don't want him to think I'm loading the whole family onto him so early in our relationship. You can understand that, can't you?" she asked anxiously.

"Oh, sure." Judy turned toward the door, already thinking about what she would wear to the party. Then a thought made her turn back abruptly. "You've told him about Larry, haven't you?"

"Well, I've told him that I have a teenage son. I haven't actually mentioned any problems with Larry. It seemed too early for that, too."

Judy frowned. "Hmmm. I suppose so. Have a good time tonight, Liza."

"You, too."

Roger cut himself shaving when he was getting ready for the party. He ran over a book he'd dropped in the garage as he pulled out. Though he'd been there before, he couldn't find Judy's building on the street of similar pairs of flats, and had to search out a phone booth to look up her address. By then he was fifteen minutes late. Though Judy waved away his profuse apologies, Roger thought perhaps it had gotten them off to a bad start for the evening.

She looked adorable in a flowing black tunic over gold and black striped pants. He'd never seen her dressed up, with her short, curly hair held back by combs and dangling earrings hanging almost to her shoulders. She didn't appear at all like his funny companion at the Russian River or the efficient, caring nurse from Six East: she seemed much more elegant and more sophisticated. Roger realized he didn't actually know her very well.

Worse, when they got to the party, she ran into someone she knew. Roger was just ushering Judy into the living room with its spectacular San Francisco backdrop, when he realized that she had caught someone's attention. Though Roger instantly identified the young man as the new cardiothoracic surgeon Fielding had hired, he could not remember his name, so he was surprised when Judy said, "Wayne. Fancy meeting you here."

Roger could not identify the edge to her voice, though he could tell there was some kind of tension between the two of them. Any idiot could have realized that. The air seemed to vibrate with it. The young surgeon shook his head wonderingly. "I knew we'd run into each other sooner or later, Judy, now that I'm going to be working at Fielding. I hope you won't mind."

Mind? Roger's gaze swung back and forth between them. Was this the Wayne Judy had spoken of?

"When did this happen?" Judy asked.

"I started on July first, just like a resident," he said with a self-deprecatory laugh. "But I understand you're not working in the OR anymore."

"No, I'm on the oncology floor." Judy, seeming to remember her manners, abruptly turned to Roger. "Roger, this is Wayne Belliver, a cardiothoracic surgeon I worked with at the General."

The young man eyed her ruefully, as though that weren't quite the description he would have given, and turned to Roger. "I think we've met, in the dressing room. It's Janek, isn't it?"

"Yes," Roger agreed, pleased that the fellow had remembered his name. "Welcome aboard, and all that."

"Thanks." The smile that flooded Wayne's features relieved them of a little of their starkness. Roger thought he looked all superimposed angles, like a Picasso drawing come to life. Belliver redirected his attention to Judy, saying, "I'd wanted to talk with you. Hear how you're doing and everything. Maybe Roger wouldn't mind if we . . ."

"Of course not," Roger said heartily, trying to be a good sport about this. "I just gave Judy a ride. We're not going to stick together all evening."

With her back turned to Wayne, she muttered, "I

thought you wanted company, Roger. Isn't that why I'm here?"

"Hey, I'm fine. You and Wayne find a quiet place to talk." He gestured toward a heavy wooden door. "There's a den there. Bound to be empty right now."

Judy looked uncertain as to whether she wanted to take advantage of a quiet den, but Wayne put a gentle, guiding hand on her shoulder and confidently led her in that direction. Roger could easily imagine the two of them as a couple. Hadn't Judy told him she'd lived with Wayne for more than a year? Roger remembered that she'd also called him a paragon of virtue, or something equally laudatory. Wayne was even, Roger had heard, a remarkably gifted surgeon. Which was probably a good thing, because he was a remarkably plain man at first sight.

After the door had closed behind the couple, Roger looked around him. He knew almost everyone in the room. Cliff and Angel were standing together near a bar that had been set up by the caterers. The head of the surgery department and his wife were talking with them, and several newly completed family-practice residents stood nearby. It would have been easy enough for Roger to join either of the groups, but he hesitated, glancing toward the den. Its door remained closed.

Behind him the front door opened to let in a fellow anesthesiologist and his woman friend, who immediately enveloped Roger with their friendliness and concern. They were the first of a stream of people who made it their business to see that he was never left alone and that he was having a good time. He was urged to eat, and to drink, and to tell some of their favorites of his stories.

An hour after he had arrived, Judy had not emerged from the den. Roger was on the verge of making up his mind to go rescue her, or reclaim her, or whatever it would be, when he noticed the door begin to open. Wayne came out, but he was not followed by Judy. Had she somehow eluded his surveillance and come out previously? Or had she departed through the other door into the hall in search of a bathroom?

Roger thought of asking Wayne what had become of Judy, but he decided against it when Wayne was immediately gobbled up by a group of Fielding surgeons who apparently wanted to make his acquaintance, or, more likely, check out for themselves his surgical credentials. People were crowded around the room with food and drinks, talking, laughing, and generally enjoying themselves. But Roger was worried because he didn't see Judy anywhere. It didn't seem likely she'd have left without telling him. And what was it with her and Wayne anyway, that they'd been in the den for so long?

Roger was about to ask Angel's advice when he saw Judy climbing the stairs from the bedroom level below. Probably the bathroom up here had been occupied, and she'd had to go downstairs to find one. There was something different about her appearance, though. Roger regarded her closely and decided that it wasn't that she'd been crying. Her cheeks were flushed, but her eyes were perfectly clear, even intense. "Did you lose your earrings?" he asked.

"No, they're in my pocket."

"Did one of them break?"

"No, they're fine. I just took them off."

"How come? I liked them."

"Roger, I just took them off, okay? I didn't want to wear them anymore."

"Did Wayne upset you?" he asked.

Judy sighed. "It wasn't Wayne, exactly. Look, Roger, I think I'll go home now, if you don't mind. I'll just call a cab."

"Hey, don't go. People are still coming. Don't let it bother you that he's here."

"It does bother me that he's here. It bothers me that he's going to be working at Fielding. It bothers me that he's getting married."

"He didn't seem to be with anyone."

"She's a surgery resident at the General, and she's on call tonight. He just told me about her."

"But you haven't been in touch with him for a long time, right?"

She made an impatient gesture with her hand. "No, it was over a very long time ago. And I'm stupid to let it bother me, but it does. What can I say, Roger?"

People were swirling around them as the house

grew more crowded. It was hardly the time or place to be discussing this, yet Roger couldn't let it go. "It's not stupid. I didn't mean that. But you can put it aside for tonight and enjoy yourself."

"Like you'd do?" she shot back, and immediately looked horrified. "I'm sorry. That was mean of me. But I feel mean, and that's why it will be better if I go home, okay?"

Roger was hurt by her comment and involuntarily stepped backward, distancing himself from her. It didn't help that she'd immediately apologized. He'd thought she understood.

His withdrawal was not lost on her. With a sad shrug she turned away from him and headed into the kitchen. Roger was torn. He didn't want to make her fend for herself, but she had seemed to make light of his pain.

Hadn't he just made light of hers? The thought had barely penetrated his consciousness when he was swept up by two fellow anesthesiologists from Fielding. "Rog, great to see you here," one of them exclaimed, clapping his hand on Roger's back. "Show us where you got that drink."

It would have been immeasurably easier to go along with them than to follow Judy. "Excuse me," he said abruptly, pointing toward the bar in the living room. "That way to the drinks. I've misplaced my date."

The two men shared a surprised look and allowed

him to slip off toward the kitchen. He found Judy there with phone in hand. "I'll take you home," he said.

She shook her head. "It's all right, Roger. I'd rather take a cab." Into the phone she said, "How long would it be?" and grimaced at the answer.

"Please," Roger urged. "I'll take you right now."

"I'm sorry," Judy said into the phone. "That's too long. Thanks anyway." When she had hung up the phone, she regarded him unhappily. "Would you come back after you drop me off?"

He shrugged. "It doesn't matter. Cliff and Angel know I've been here. I've put in an appearance."

"They wanted you to come so you'd enjoy yourself, not to please them." But she moved away from the phone toward him. "I'm sorry I was so nasty out there."

"I'm sorry I was so callous. I guess I've gotten to thinking I'm the only one in the world who has problems. Which is hard to comprehend when I do the kind of work I do. I'm not proud of it."

"Oh, Roger." Judy gave him a quick hug. "You're about the nicest person I know."

Startled, he shook his head. "You're confusing me with someone else."

"I don't think so. Look how good you've been about Larry, and how patient you were when my car got the flat. And all that after you've had such a hard year. Anyway, if you really don't mind, I'd like you to drive me home. And then I hope you'll come back to the party."

"Maybe." As they left the kitchen Roger decided it would be too difficult to speak with Angel and Cliff. He could call them tomorrow if he didn't come back.

The sounds of party gaiety followed them to the door and beyond. The familiar voices, the laughter, the music, and the smells of food filled the night with a special warmth. If Kerri hadn't been sick when Roger married her, they would have entertained their friends like this. At the end of the evening they would have kicked off their shoes and sat down on a sofa, exhausted, to discuss the success of their endeavors.

Roger realized that Judy, who had probably thought herself fully recovered and immune to any sadness or regret, had tonight unexpectedly been reminded of what might have been. Judy had undoubtedly loved that angular fellow, Wayne, and thought that one day the two of them would give parties for their friends. Now, instead, he had reappeared in her life, and would stay a presence in it because of his new job at Fielding, only to inform her that he was marrying someone else.

Friends would welcome Wayne's new bride and share the happy couple's hospitality. People would comment on their affection for each other and how they were a great couple. Didn't everyone love seeing Angel and Cliff together? It was an affirmation that good happened, that two people, disparate as they might be, could live together and love each other and start a family.

Judy had probably envisioned those same things for herself and Wayne at one time. What did it matter that that had been a few years ago? Nothing had come into her life since then to substitute for that special kind of relationship. Living with her sister and her nephew was hardly the same thing. Roger thought Judy must miss that singular attraction between a man and a woman as much as he did.

The air was chilly, and neither of them had worn jackets. Fog clung to these middle reaches of Twin Peaks, and he saw Judy shiver slightly. "I'll get the heat on in the car right away," he promised as he held the door for her.

"Thanks," she said as she slid into the Audi's passenger seat.

"I should know San Francisco's weather better after all these years."

"Yeah, me, too."

When he started up the Audi and flipped on the heater, a blast of cold air shocked both of them. Roger turned it off instantly, but cold air continued to pour upward from the floor, making him feel chilled to the bone. "Geez!" he complained, tugging at various knobs and switches. "I don't mean to freeze you. I just can't seem to . . ."

Judy wrapped her arms around herself, the filmy tunic shivering along with her flesh. "Turn it to defrost."

"Huh?" But Roger did as she suggested, and the freezing air abated. "God, I'm sorry."

"That's all right."

Afterward he would not be able to explain to himself just why he did it. She looked so cold, and so sad, and so lonely, but that was hardly an excuse. He turned to her and took her in his arms—to warm her. Her look of stunned surprise didn't escape him, but when he was holding her tightly against him, he could no longer see her face. He could only feel her body pressed against his, her breasts compacted on his chest. "Is that better?" he asked. "Does that warm you up a little?"

There was a muffled "yes" against his shirt, and she made no effort to draw back from him. He rubbed his hands up and down on her back and then her arms, like a skier trying to generate some heat.

And Roger remembered what it had been like at the Russian River in bed with Judy. He remembered how he'd curled his body against her and how he'd wanted her. And he wanted her now. He wanted her warmth and her generosity and her enticing body. He wanted to touch her flesh. He wanted their bare bodies pressed against each other.

"Judy?"

What could she possibly be thinking of him?

"I need you, Judy," slipped from his mouth before he could stop it. "God, I'm sorry. I have no right to say that to you."

Her voice came muffled against his shirt. "Right now, I want you, too, Roger. But it will pass, won't it? Like at the bed-and-breakfast."

"Sure," he said, not letting go of her. The car was warmer now. He could no longer feel her shiver. But he could no more take his hands away from her than he could drive her home. Roger kissed her temple, the springy curls feeling alive and tempting to his lips. He whispered into them, "I don't think it's going to go away, Judy."

For a long moment she said nothing. Then gradually she lifted her face and tentatively touched her lips to his. He responded gently at first, and then more passionately. His whole body had caught fire. He knew this was Judy, and he knew what he was doing was going to make him feel bad tomorrow, but tonight he needed her. And, for what it was worth, he could tell she needed him, too.

"Could I take you to my house?" he asked, his voice raw with his desire. "Would that be all right with you?"

"Oh, Roger." He could see the struggle in her face, the battle with reason. Although he despised himself for doing it, even then, he kissed her again with all the urgency of his need. His hand moved to cup her breast through the filmy tunic and her bra. His thumb strayed over her nipple. She sighed and said, "Okay. I want this, too."

Roger told himself that they could change their

minds as he drove across San Francisco. He told himself that they *would* change their minds. He was a recent widower, and she was a woman who had just been reminded of a failed love affair. He drove the banged-up Audi cautiously down Twin Peaks and across Corbett to Ashbury and Masonic. He could think of nothing to say to Judy. Afraid that anything he would say would indeed make them rethink their decision, he preferred to say nothing at all.

Judy sat beside him, her body huddled slightly against heaven knew what, since the car was perfectly warm now. If she was trying to get up the courage to ask him to take her to her flat, there was as yet no evidence. Her hands lay clasped tightly in her lap. Her eyes stayed locked on the ever-changing scene in front of the car. Her breathing seemed slightly more rapid and shaky than normal.

They got every red light possible as they crossed toward Laurel Heights. At each intersection where they had to pause, he glanced questioningly at her, but she didn't meet his gaze. If she had, he knew she would have said something like, "This is not a good idea, Roger." But she didn't speak, and each time the light turned green he continued in the direction of his own house. Finally, on California Street just a few blocks away, he said, "Are you sure, Judy?"

"No, of course I'm not sure. No more than you are." She reached her left hand out to lay it possessively on his right thigh. "Tonight this is what we need. Maybe tomorrow we'll be sorry. That doesn't make me not want to go ahead tonight."

"I know. I want to make love with you, Judy, right now."

He had his blinker on for the right-hand turn. Judy drew her hand back abruptly from his leg. "I don't have any birth control, Roger."

A lump formed instantly in his throat. He could picture the box of condoms in the nightstand. There for how long? Did they go bad? He had bought them, he remembered vividly, so that no additional stress would be put on Kerri's body. Almost, he felt he couldn't take Judy there. To that house, to that bedroom, to that bed. But he wanted her so badly, his loins ached with his desire.

"I have what we need."

He swung the car onto Cherry Street and drove the two blocks in silence. In the dark cold night the garage door rattled slowly up as they waited in the driveway. There was one light on in the house, in the living room behind the drawn curtains. Roger pulled the car into the garage and came around to open the door for Judy. As she stepped out of the car, he took her into his arms and held her tightly against him, his face buried in her fresh-scented hair. "Thank you for coming."

"I didn't do it for you," she said.

But Roger wondered, momentarily. And then he took her hand and drew her toward the basement door.

Chapter Ten

Judy had never been in Roger's house. She was aware, although not sure how, that he had owned it for several years, and that after Kerri died he had not been able to stay there after a while. He had lived with Angel's old roommate Nan for several months before recently returning to the house on Cherry Street. It was a lovely neighborhood, with wonderful old and elegant houses, Roger's not the least of them.

As he led her through the house, she caught glimpses of a living and dining room on the main floor, before they started to climb the stairs. Roger stopped abruptly and turned toward her. "I'm being a boor," he announced. "I could at least get you a drink, or we could have a cup of tea or something."

"It's not necessary." It's not even a good idea, she thought, if we're going to go through with this. In some ways Judy felt like a twenty-year-old virgin. This was something she wanted to do, but she very much suspected that given a chance to rethink her situation, or to think much at all, she would have the wisdom to call a halt to their headlong rush into bed.

Roger nodded and continued the climb upward, her hand still tight in his. At the head of the stairs he hesitated, not, she felt sure, because he didn't know where his bedroom was, but because he wasn't sure he wanted to take her there. Then, a look of determination on his face, he turned to the right and preceded her into what was obviously the master suite.

There was an enormous king-size bed in the middle of the room, with oak headboard and nightstands on either side. There were oak bookcases on two of the walls, and a carpet so thick it was noticeable. Judy kicked off her shoes so she could sink her toes into the velvety burgundy nap. The bedspread was gray, with a trim of burgundy, matching pillowcases and flounce. Judy suspected Roger had someone in to clean because the place was immaculate, except for his clothes scattered around the room.

The clothes were oddly comforting. Certainly he hadn't expected to bring anyone back here with him tonight, or they wouldn't be gracing the floor and one of the chairs. They were probably the clothes he'd worn to work today, and they seemed familiar, as if she'd seen him earlier in the day wearing them.

Roger gave a tsk of annoyance and tossed the lot of them behind an open closet door, which he closed with his knee.

There was an awkward moment then, when they stood together in the middle of the large room. He looked a little lost, a little wary, even though it was his own house. Judy met his gaze with a straightforward one of her own. This was not a time to allow her own doubts to surface. She lifted a hand to run it tentatively through his curly hair, and he kissed the inside of her wrist. Instantly she felt the tug of sexual attraction, and she stood on tiptoe to kiss him.

His kisses were unequivocal. There was nothing tentative about them at all. This was a man who knew what he wanted, and who was, with his mouth, very persuasive indeed. He knew how to seduce with his lips, and with his tongue. For a long time it was only his mouth that touched her, nibbling, tasting, urging, until Judy wanted nothing more than to be already naked and wound tightly against him. Her heart pounded and her knees felt wobbly.

Long after she was ready for him to do so his hands moved between them to caress her breasts. A sigh of satisfaction escaped her lips and into his mouth. "Mmm," he said. "You taste like heaven."

Her tunic floated all the way down to her knees, but the fabric was so filmy that it escaped his intention at first. "How do you get this thing off?" he grumbled. "It's hiding too much of you."

Judy stepped back and lifted it off from the shoulders, with his help. She was left standing in front of him in a black bra and the black and gold pants. He reached around to unhook the bra. With a slight tug he removed it and flung it across the room. "I knew you'd be beautiful," he whispered. "Lying beside you at the Russian River I wanted so much to see you. I never thought it would happen."

"Don't leave me naked alone. It embarrasses me."

Immediately Roger began to strip off his shirt. "It shouldn't. It's just me, and I think you look wonderful." Once he had started removing his clothes, he simply went ahead and did the whole job, not a modest or shy bone in his body. He stood before her naked, already aroused and comfortable with himself. He was as wiry as she'd suspected, all that trapped energy ready to exert itself in pleasing the two of them.

His hands came again to cup her breasts, and his head bowed to take one nipple in his mouth. She could feel the tug all the way down to her womb, urging her to take him into her, to fill the need that continued to grow. His hand slid down inside her pants, down to the curly hair, and farther. A finger touched her most sensitive spot, and she moaned.

"Here. Let's get you out of these unnecessary clothes," he suggested, running his hands down her sides and taking the pants and underpants with them. In a moment she stood before him as naked as he, and he drew her to him, pressing their bodies together, his penis thumping a counter-rhythm to the beat of her heart.

Once again his lips came to hers with their urgency and temptation. She felt herself walked backward toward the bed, and when her knees touched, she reached down to pull back the bedspread and sheet. Their eyes met, and he said, "You get in bed. I'll get a condom."

From the unfamiliar bed she watched him open the nightstand drawer. He took out a packet and turned on the bedside light, a beam of high intensity by which he must usually read. He snapped off the overhead light and covered the bright light with a blue shirt that he plucked from the floor. A gauzy glow was cast over the room. Judy even watched as he opened the packet and donned the condom, for some reason finding the experience only heightened her anticipation.

And then he was beside her, leaving the covers at the bottom of the bed. "I want to be able to see you," he said. "Is that okay?"

"I guess so." Judy guessed everything was okay when his lips came again to kiss her breast. Her arms went around him, stroking the skin at his waist and then his buttocks. His firmness thrilled her in a way that made her throat tighten with need. Gently, his finger slid down her belly and through the triangle of coarse hair, pausing only briefly.

Because of the insistent tug of his lips at her breast, she felt the ache gather strength. And when his finger slid farther down, softly coaxing that swelling bud into flower, Judy gasped with the intensity. Roger sighed with pleasure as she ran her hands down the backs of his legs, drawing herself closer to him. Their bodies lay skin on skin, with a heightened sensitivity that scarcely seemed possible. He switched from one breast to the other, drawing on her sweetly yet with real urgency.

And the bud between her legs seemed like the most exotic flower, too special to have peeked out so spectacularly ever before. A slippery finger slid inside her, and she groaned. "Please, Roger."

"Soon," he whispered. His tongue wound around her breast, flicking at the nipple. "Let me just taste this a little longer."

The combination of the pull at her breast and the urgency at her womb nearly made her faint with desire. She ran her hand between his legs and along the shaft of his penis, stroked him, locked her thumb and middle finger in a circle around him, and squeezed him forward and back, tempting, teasing, hoping to build his need to her level, so that he would be unable to wait a moment longer.

He laughed, a deep, rich sound right at her breast, and indeed along the length of her. "Yes, I want you and I can hardly stand it," he admitted. "But there's something I want from you first."

"What?" she asked, barely able to speak. Her lips were dry, her mouth caught in his hair as he sucked on her. "Anything."

"You'll know," he sighed against her flesh. His finger slid from inside her right up along the bursting bud, and his penis came to follow the same route, rubbing, teasing her. But not sinking deeply into her yet, just tormenting her desire.

Which built higher, and impossibly higher. "Oh, Roger," she gasped, as all hell broke loose in her body. "Oh, God."

"That's what I wanted." And he lost himself in her as she clasped him in her arms. He moved in such a way that she felt a shock of realization that her orgasm was not fading, but still rolling in joyous waves of pleasure. He kissed her as he rose and fell, smiling into her face and shifting slightly with each stroke. Judy could scarcely believe how he was prolonging her delight while he carefully controlled his own final explosion.

A bubble of laughter grew in her until she laughed out loud with sheer exuberance. As if it were a signal, he seemed to reach the peak of his enjoyment and came with a shuddering intensity that touched her deeply. If she weren't so giggly with elation, she would have felt like weeping for the obviously necessary release he was experiencing.

And then he cried out in a new and different way that frightened her. His face paled with agony and he slumped down on her, and Judy thought for a moment that he'd had a heart attack. Impossible, of course, but what else could have happened?

His breath came in awkward pants. "Oh, shit!"

"What is it? What can I do?" Naked, frightened, Judy tried to roll away from him but was trapped under the weight of his body. When she shifted he cried out in pain. "What's happening, Roger?"

Between clenched teeth, he said, "It's my back. Jesus! I can't move."

Judy forced herself out from under him, since she had no option. His muffled scream told her the movement was not without consequence. He lay now on his back on the bed, his face a grimace of pain, his extremities spread-eagled helplessly at his sides, the condom still on his penis. "Has this happened before?" she asked as she eased herself out of the large bed.

"No. Never. My back is perfectly okay. At least it has been." He groaned. "Oh, God. I'm not going to be able to take you home. You can take my car."

"I'm not going anywhere yet." Judy rose from the bed and quickly drew on her clothes.

He lay on the bed, his eyes closed, and she could tell that a back spasm took him as he gritted his teeth and muttered, "Oh, shit." She returned to the bed, feeling helpless. "What can I get you in the way of medication, Roger? Ibuprofen?"

"There's a box in the linen closet in the hall with

aspirin and painkillers and other stuff. Maybe you could bring that, and I'll see what I have. And a glass of water."

It was only when she was returning with her hands full that she noticed the picture of Kerri. The photo was at least eight by ten, in a gold frame, of a healthy, smiling Kerri, the picture taken against an outdoor setting. It rested on the bedside table farthest from where she set down the cardboard box and the glass of water. Had he noticed the picture when they were making love?

The box itself had a dozen different prescription drugs in it, and most of them had Kerri's name on them. Well, Roger was a doctor, an anesthesiologist. He would surely know what kind of pain medication to take. Judy thought he looked so vulnerable lying there naked that she removed the condom and eased the covers out from under him, pulling them up to his waist before she set the box within his reach. "See what you can find," she suggested. "And you're not going to be able to sit up to drink, so I'll see if there's a straw somewhere downstairs. Okay?"

"Judy, I hate to ask you to do this. I just can't move."

In his eyes, in his face, she saw a combination of pain, fear, sorrow, helplessness, and maybe other confused emotions as well. She reached down to touch his forehead and brush the hair back. "I know, Roger. It's no problem. I'll look downstairs."

It felt strange, wandering around the unfamiliar house at night. In the kitchen there was another picture, this one of Kerri and Roger, taken at their wedding in the hospital. Judy remembered being there, of even taking part in preparing for the unusual event. She tried to remember how she'd felt about Roger at the time, but she only remembered a distant knowledge of him, with his buoyant optimism and boundless energy. His insistence on the wedding had seemed to fly in the face of reason, and yet to be perfectly in keeping with his personality.

But as she dug through drawers of flatwear and kitchen utensils and pot holders and pans looking for a straw, she remembered mostly thinking what a lucky man Roger was. Kerri had been a very special woman—courageous, thoughtful, loving. Judy had known that Kerri would help Roger accustom himself to her death, rather than the other way around. And sure enough, Kerri had enlisted Angel Crawford's help to stand by Roger when she inevitably succumbed to her illness.

Not that Roger had proved such an easy person to console. Maybe his despair had been in direct proportion to the joy he'd known with his love. Judy felt a stab of pain herself at the thought and rummaged more aggressively in the most likely drawer. Under bottle openers and fancy skewers, she found two straws with flexible necks. "Perfect," she murmured to herself, straightening. For a long moment she stood in the kitchen, trying to sort out her own emotions, but found the exercise impossible. For now, she thought, I'll be his nurse. That's what he needs.

When she came back into the bedroom, he turned his head toward her and attempted to smile. "You've found one. I wasn't sure I had any." He patted the bed beside him. "Here. Sit down a minute. I don't want you to wait on me."

"Well, you'll just have to put up with it," she said, remaining where she was. "I'm going to be Nurse Judy for a while now, Roger, and accumulate a few things you'll need—like a cane or a stick to help you get out of bed."

"I'm never going to get out of bed again."

"You wish. In about an hour you'll need to use the bathroom, and you're not going to be able to manage without a cane."

He grimaced. "I think there's one in the hall closet downstairs. Judy, I'm sorry. I didn't . . . I feel so stupid."

"Don't. It's not necessary. You're not in control of when your back goes out."

"But we were . . . You must think I wish we hadn't made love . . . or something. But I don't." Roger was wracked with a spasm that made him grit out a pained "Oh, shit" again.

"Maybe you do, unconsciously," Judy suggested, finally seating herself on the side of the bed. "I realize it's not an intentional thing, Roger. We both got carried away, for different reasons, and maybe they don't have enough to do with each other. It's all right. We'll forget what happened, okay?"

He looked miserable, but reluctantly nodded.

With brusque efficiency Judy bent the straw and placed it in his glass of water. "Did you find something for the pain?"

"Yeah." He popped a pill in his mouth and allowed her to hold the glass for him to take a sip. When he had finished, Judy put the glass on the bedside table and stood up.

"I'll find the cane."

This time when she returned, he had painfully turned himself over and was struggling to reach something on the floor beside the bed. "Don't do that," she said sharply. "I'll get you whatever you need."

There was sweat on his forehead from the effort. "My keys. You can drive the Audi home, unless you'd prefer a cab."

Judy sighed. "I'm not going home, Roger. I can't very well leave you here alone in this condition. What if you fell when you tried to go to the bathroom?" She motioned with her head to the room across the hall. "I'll sleep there, and you'll just need to yell if you need something. In the morning we can discuss what to do, but you should try to get some sleep now. And don't try to argue with me. You're in no position to argue."

"Maybe it will be all better in the morning," he said hopefully, though they both knew that it wouldn't. "Thanks, Judy. You're a brick."

The room opposite his was much smaller and a bit sterile as far as furnishings went. A bed, a chair, a bureau, and an old television were the sum total of its accoutrements. Judy left the door open and shed her pants and top, pulled down the dull gold bedspread and climbed into the bed. She felt suddenly exhausted, as if she'd spent the last few hours hiking in the mountains.

Undoubtedly, she should have stayed home, as she'd originally planned. Nothing had gone right, except for that brief period when Roger had held her in his arms. And look what the aftermath of that had been. Well, she should have known better. How could she have let herself get into that kind of situation in the first place? Judy thumped the pillow with an impotent fist, sank her head into it, and fell asleep.

Roger managed, with several bouts of excruciating pain, to get himself to the bathroom early the next morning. He could see Judy through the open door of the guest room, sound asleep, and he would have called her if he'd needed to, but he made it there and back without anything drastic happening. When he returned, he lowered himself to the bed, in agony, and sprawled back, totally fatigued. Sleep eluded him, though, as dawn spread outside his window.

Birds sang in the nearby trees, and an occasional car whisked by on the street. Roger thought of the mornings he'd woken up in that bed beside Kerri when it was she who was in pain. Always she had managed a smile and a warm greeting, as though his presence were some special kind of gift, like bird-song or sunshine.

How many times had he tried to stay home with her when she'd given him a little push, saying, "Out, out. You have a job to do, Dr. Janek. Patients need you. Surgeons depend on you. Fielding Medical Center can't manage without you. I'll be fine. Andrea (or Joan or Lucy or Carol) is coming by to spend the day with me." And he had gone, reluctantly, heavy-hearted, always afraid that she would somehow slip through his fingers that day.

But it hadn't happened like that. She'd died in her sleep, right there beside him. Sometimes he'd wondered if she'd awoken and known she was dying, if she'd tried to get his attention, to ask for his help. But this morning he knew she hadn't. He *knew* she'd just let go in her sleep, left him softly, undramatically. That was Kerri. And she was gone forever. He had been fighting this whole past year to hold onto her, when she was already gone.

Roger slept then, for several hours, only to be awakened by the loud ringing of the phone. Last night he had automatically turned the answering machine off, but now he found that the phone was too far away from his spot on the bed for him to reach it without intolerable pain. Afraid that the ringing would wake Judy, though, he tried to roll over, to reach as far as his arm would go, but he was not successful. The phone stopped ringing, and he slumped back helplessly on the bed.

Almost immediately it started to ring again, and again he pulled himself slowly and painfully toward the other side of the bed where the phone remained just out of his reach on the bedside table. It rang and rang. Who the hell was so intent on getting hold of him?

"Lie still!" he heard Judy order him. "I'll get it for you."

She was dressed only in bra and underpants, and looked half asleep as she stumbled across to pick up the receiver and stop the infernal ringing. Without saying anything into it, she handed it across to him and walked quickly from the room.

"Hello?"

"Roger? Is something the matter?"

It was Angel, and her voice was filled with concern.

"Well," he said cautiously, "my back's gone out."

"Your back? But you looked fine last night. Did it happen at the party? Is that why you left early?"

"No, it happened when I got home." That was true enough.

"How bad is it, Roger? Can you walk?"

"No," he admitted. "I mean, I can if I have to, but it would be foolish to do anything but stay in bed. It's very painful."

"Poor dear! I'll come right over and set you up. Do you need any painkillers or muscle relaxants?"

"No, I've got everything I need."

"But if you can't move . . ."

"Someone's here."

"Someone's there?" Angel sounded confused. "But who? Did you call someone? Why didn't you call us?"

"She was here," Roger said. "Everything's under control, Angel."

He could hear Cliff in the background, pestering Angel with questions as she repeated the information Roger was giving her. There was a break in their conversation while enlightenment seemed to spring on both of them. Quite distinctly he heard Cliff say, "The poor guilt-ridden bastard! Here, let me talk to him."

Chapter Eleven

Roger gritted his teeth and said, "I'm not a guilt-ridden bastard, Cliff. My back went out. That's all."

"Oh, sure, sure," his friend said. "Look, we're talking Judy here, are we?"

"It's none of your business. But yes. And I don't want you or Angel flying over here to wipe my fevered brow. I'll be fine."

"I wouldn't think of wiping your brow or anything else," Cliff assured him. "Look, Roger, I know it's been hard for you since Kerri died. I don't blame you for being sad and retreating from things a bit. But I miss you being the way you used to be, you know? Someone I could tease and dump on and yell at."

"Gosh, me, too," Roger replied with sufficient sarcasm to make Cliff laugh. "I'm getting there, Cliff. I moved back into my house, didn't I? Just give me time."

"You've got all the time you need, old fellow. I just wish I'd get a chance to see the old you before we leave for Wisconsin. But, hell, that's nothing. Is . . . uh . . . Judy there right now?"

"Sort of." Roger could hear her in the bathroom across the hall. "She slept in the guest room."

"No wonder. Well, look, if you need anything later, give us a call. We'll be around, packing and such. If Angel just feels the urge to come by and see you, I'll make sure she calls first."

"Thanks."

Judy appeared at the bedroom door as Roger depressed the button on the receiver. She was dressed in the tunic and pants now, and looked slightly embarrassed. "Did you thank them for the party?" she asked.

"No, I didn't remember. Look, Judy, you don't have to hang around. Take the Audi. I'm certainly not going to need it for a couple days."

"You haven't had any breakfast," she protested. "A good nurse never leaves her patient starving. I thought I could bring you a bowl of cereal and leave you with something to drink and crackers to munch on later. You're not going to be able to get up and down the stairs, Roger."

Food was the last thing on his mind. He just wanted her to be gone so that he could suffer alone.

He didn't want them to be in this embarrassing situation. He had made a fool of himself, and he had used her. Hadn't he? He was not, after all, in the habit of sleeping with women he scarcely knew. But he had wanted her so badly last night. He had needed to hold her and arouse her and satisfy her. He had needed her to want him, too.

Roger frowned at her. "Cliff thinks that I'm—and I quote—'a poor guilt-ridden bastard.' "

Judy moved farther into the room and stood uneasily on one foot. "You probably are, Roger. Guilt-ridden, I mean. But sex isn't that big a deal, really. At least most people don't seem to think so. We've already decided to forget it, remember? And maybe you shouldn't have told Dr. Lenzini."

"I didn't exactly tell them," Roger grumbled. "In fact, I was trying not to, but they seemed to jump to that conclusion. I'm sure they won't tell anyone. And besides, they're leaving for Wisconsin in a few days."

Roger wanted to say that he didn't want to forget their sexual encounter, but he didn't have the energy to explain what he meant. His back had just begun to spasm again, and he clenched the bedclothes to relieve the helpless pain. When it had stopped, he tried to smile at her worried expression.

"They only last a moment. Not like when I move. Yes, do bring me up some food, if you would. If you'd just leave a pile of stuff—maybe my briefcase, too. And some magazines from the living room, and the mystery I was reading. God, don't I sound demanding? But if I'm going to be stuck up here alone . . ." His voice dwindled away. He hoped he didn't sound as pathetic as he felt.

Judy moved briskly to the door. "Just call me Cherry Ames," she said over her shoulder as she strode down the hall.

Half an hour later the bed was stocked with food, reading material, work, a laptop computer, the telephone, and the morning's paper. Judy had left after he'd finished the cereal, which he'd eaten from a bowl placed on his chest. Very inconvenient, but better than having her feed him. She set out a pair of pajamas for him, flannel ones that he kept for the cabin, but he hadn't had the energy or the nerve to try to get them on yet. "I'll manage," he'd assured her.

She had promised to call later to check on him. Roger had had to force himself not to say "Please don't bother." It wasn't that he didn't want to hear from her. He was afraid it wasn't a good idea. And he hated himself for thinking that. None of this was her fault. And yet, if it weren't for her, he wouldn't have slept with someone last night—and betrayed Kerri's memory, right here in their bed.

A stupid way to think, maybe, but he couldn't help himself. He was indeed a poor guilt-ridden bastard, as Cliff had said.

* * *

Liza was washing windows in the kitchen when Judy came in. Larry's door was closed, suggesting that he wasn't even awake yet. Judy had been surprised to find that it was only ten when she left Roger's. Liza looked up from her work with a teasing, provocative expression. "And you didn't even want to go to the party," she said.

"Don't ask." Judy tugged open the refrigerator door and helped herself to a diet Coke. "Wayne was there."

Liza looked shocked. "Surely you didn't spend the night with Wayne!"

"No, no, of course not." Judy dug through the vegetable bin and came up with an Asian pear. She hadn't taken the time to eat at Roger's, since it was obvious that he wanted her out of his house. "Wayne told me he's getting married. I guess it threw me a little. The two of us were finished a long time ago, but it sounds so final, marriage. And it means there's some woman that he did fall in love with. A doctor. A resident at the General. Might have known."

"He didn't seem to feel there was any problem with your being a nurse," Liza protested. "Doctors marry nurses all the time."

"And live to regret it, I'm coming to believe. We're not sophisticated enough for them."

"Does this have something to do with Roger? Did you spend the night with Roger?"

Judy pursed her lips. "Well, in a manner of speaking. I certainly spent the night at Roger's house."

"Don't make me pull it out of you, Judy. What happened?"

"I guess we were both feeling lonely and abandoned. And there was that physical attraction sort of still clinging to us from the night at the Russian River." Judy felt again the strength of that attraction and sighed. Keeping her eyes trained on the pear, she said, "We did go to bed together. But right afterward, all of a sudden his back went out and he was in incredible pain. He wanted me to leave, I think, but that wasn't reasonable with him in that condition. So I spent the night in the guest room and set him up this morning with what he'll need for a while."

"Why did he want you to leave?"

Judy shrugged. "I'm not sure. I think he regretted what we'd done, and I think he felt vulnerable not being able to move. But it was more than that." She sliced off a bite of pear and crunched it thoughtfully. "I'm sure it's all wound up with Kerri dying, but I don't know precisely how."

"Do you regret it?"

Judy stared out the clean window, a faraway look in her eyes. For a long time she didn't speak. Finally, she said, "No, I don't regret it. But we've agreed to forget it happened and just go back to the way we were before."

Liza's expression became rueful. "And how was that, Judy?"

"We were friends, my dear, just friends."

"That doesn't work so well, going backward. Most people can't manage it."

"Yeah, I know. Roger will be able to. I don't know about me."

They heard the sounds of a teenager thumping down the hall, and Larry appeared in the kitchen doorway, his spiky hair rumpled from a night's sleep and the stubble of several days without shaving on his chin. "So what's up?" he asked, looking suspiciously from one to the other of them.

"Nothing much," his mother replied, returning to her window washing. "I want you to pick up your room this morning before you go out."

"Roger may need your help, too," Judy said. "His back's gone out. I have the Audi."

"Yeah? Can I drive it?" he asked with a grin. "I've got it running pretty well, haven't I?"

"Not bad. But you'll have to ask Roger about driving it. He's a trusting soul."

Larry had taken a carton of milk from the refrigerator and was about to lift it to his mouth when both his aunt and his mother said, "Use a glass!"

"That is such a waste," he grumbled, reaching into the cabinet above the sink. "Then you just have to wash it."

"Then *you* just have to wash it," his mother amended.

Larry raised his eyes heavenward and poured a full glass, which was drained in less than a minute. "When can I ask Roger about the Audi?"

"Later," Judy said as she rose. "This afternoon."

If Roger had thought that it was going to be a quick process, the healing of his back, he was soon disillusioned. He had fallen asleep for several hours that morning and awoke wondering if things were better. One simple attempt to roll over on his side was enough to convince him that they weren't. How the hell was he going to manage? Crackers might keep him from starving, but he could hardly picture living on them for several days. And getting downstairs was simply too big a project to even contemplate today. Maybe tomorrow, or the next day.

His miserable helplessness was at its peak when the phone rang and Judy asked him how he was getting on.

"I feel like shit," he confessed. "But I'll be fine. I don't want you worrying about me."

"No, I can see that you don't, but I have a suggestion. How about letting Larry drive the Audi and do some errands for you? Pick up a hamburger or a pizza, take care of things around the house. Just until you're better."

"That doesn't seem fair to him."

"Well, ask. He'd love driving the car, and he could work off some of those community service hours. Besides, he's never really seen anyone incapacitated, and it will be good training for his career in emergency medical services."

"Oh, great. I can be a lesson. Such an appealing thought. Is he there? I could ask him."

Without saying good-bye, Judy passed the phone to her nephew, who agreed to the project with alacrity. Roger could just imagine what the boy would do with the Audi. But, hell, it was a better solution than he'd been able to come up with so far. "How about coming at one and bringing a sausage pizza?" he said.

When he had hung up, Roger wondered how the boy was going to let himself in, but fell asleep before he could worry about it.

Judy worked Sunday, a day when almost nothing seemed to go right. She had too many patients to feel she was doing her best for each of them, and one of her patients was in severe pain from the final stages of cancer. The resident refused to order more pain medication for her patient even on Judy's specific recommendation. While she realized that the patient's tolerance for medication had gotten so high the resident was fearful of being censured for prescribing too large dosages, Judy's concern was for the comfort of her patient.

After once more being approached by the patient's

son, who could scarcely stand to see his mother in such pain, Judy finally searched down and confronted the resident in a room reserved for the doctors across from the nurses' station. "Mrs. Winslow has to have more pain medication, George. I need you to order it now."

The resident, a cocky man in his second year of surgical training, shook his head. "She's getting enough, Judy. Any more will kill her."

"It won't kill her if she needs it, and she's terminal in any case. She's in severe pain, George. It's been documented in her chart every shift. Have you been in to see her recently?"

"I saw her this morning, and my judgment is that she's only in mild discomfort."

"Even if that were true, there's no reason for her to be in any discomfort. Her family is frantic for us to do something to relieve her pain. The nurses have commented on it in her chart. Have you seen their notes?"

"I can see with my own eyes, Povalski, and I'm telling you she's okay."

The young man attempted to end their discussion by turning away, but Judy refused to let the matter rest. "I've been working on the oncology unit for several years now. I've spent more than two minutes a shift with Mrs. Winslow, and I know she's in severe pain. She's exhibiting pain behavior of the highest order. Granted she's one of those people whose tolerance for morphine has become exceptionally high, but that's no reason why we shouldn't be able to keep her relatively comfortable. She's not going to get addicted, George. She's dying."

"And any more morphine would depress her respirations to an unacceptable level, Judy. We don't do euthanasia here at Fielding."

"No, but we try to strive for some kind of balance. Relieving her pain is the only thing we can do for Mrs. Winslow now, and we're not doing it."

At the best of times Judy would not have wanted this particular kind of discussion overheard by any of the other medical or nursing staff. When she saw a movement at the doorway, she glanced up and her heart thumped unpleasantly. Wayne stood there in green surgical scrubs, a chart in one hand. She could tell, by his expression, that he had overheard some of their comments. Much as she wanted to simply walk away from the situation, she could not in good conscience do that until she had played her final card.

With a minimal nod to Wayne, she turned back to George and said softly, "It's my responsibility to see that my patient gets sufficient medication. If you won't do it, I'll have to go through the proper channels to see that it's done."

George had no intention of losing face by giving in. "You won't do that."

Wayne had not gone away, much as she'd hoped he would. Instead he advanced into the small, well-lit room and set his chart on the counter. As if he had every right to be a part of the conversation, he said, "Tell me what the procedure is here for a nurse in these circumstances, Judy. What will you have to do?"

"I'll report the problem to my nursing supervisor, and if that doesn't bring a solution, to the patient's attending doctor. Both of them will have to assess the patient themselves before making a decision."

"That sounds reasonable," Wayne admitted. He turned to the young man, who was regarding him with hostility. "I don't think we've met yet. I'm Wayne Belliver, the new associate professor of surgery. Cardiothoracic. We didn't meet at the Lenzinis the other night, did we? I saw Judy there, but I met so many other people I haven't quite gotten them down yet."

Very smoothly done, Judy thought, remembering Wayne's facility for handling people. George probably hadn't been invited, but there was no need for him to say so, and Wayne's assumption that a second-year resident would have been there was kind in any case. She watched George offer his hand with a minimum of fuss.

"Would you object to my coming with the two of you to see the patient? Between the three of us we could probably speed up this process." Shepherding the two of them out before himself, he continued talking about the point system that had been adopted at San Francisco General to assess pain, and how useful it was proving.

Judy and George, who both knew he had absolutely no right to interpose himself into the situation, nonetheless hesitated to tell him so. Wayne was such an overpoweringly *good* person that people simply could not resist his efforts. She'd seen it over and over when she worked in the operating room with him. Other surgeons had attempted to cut him down by insinuating that he was a wimp and a goody-two-shoes, but they never made the least headway. People *liked* Wayne. They never doubted his good intentions, or, in fact, his ability to remedy almost any situation. Plus he was a hell of a surgeon, and his patients loved him.

Judy led the way into Mrs. Winslow's room, where her patient lay in bed with her eyes closed, softly moaning with pain. Her son and daughter-in-law were standing close to the bed, each gently massaging one of her hands. Wayne stepped forward and introduced himself as Dr. Belliver, who had "come to learn about the patient's problem."

Young Mr. Winslow looked hopeful as he wrung Wayne's hand. "Good of you to come, Doctor. My mother is suffering terribly."

Without appearing to take any position other than the outsider eager to understand the entire situation, Wayne began to ask questions: of the patient Mrs. Winslow, of her son and his wife, of George, and of

Judy. Because of his remarkable ability to strain partisanship and overwrought emotion from a situation and leave only the glaring bare bones, he had soon reached a point of comprehension usually reserved for someone who had been working with a case for many months.

"Excellent," he said at length. Already his plain face and oversize ears were disappearing in the view of his audience, who all seemed singularly eager to please him. Mrs. Winslow smiled for the first time in many days as he took her hand.

Wayne returned her smile with an angelic one of his own. "You understand that more morphine could possibly shorten your life, your son understands it, and your daughter-in-law understands it. You also know that more medication in order to be strong enough to control your pain may take away your clarity of mind, although that won't necessarily happen."

The three laypeople nodded their agreement. Wayne turned to George. "I can understand your concerns, Dr. Carruthers. There are matters of ethics and principle involved here. I would never insist that a doctor act against his conscience in cases like this, so if you would care to consider me a consult I would be happy to write orders for additional medication."

Silver-tongued genius, Judy thought, with every effort to restrain any sign of having gotten her way. George had come quickly to see that Mrs. Winslow was, indeed, in great pain, and the longer they stayed in the room the more he understood. Unfortunately, doctors often only came into a patient's room, especially the room of a dying patient, for very brief periods of time, and then the patient was often on best behavior, not indicating how much distress they were suffering.

George manfully agreed that Mrs. Winslow needed more medication and that he was ready to prescribe it. He and Wayne excused themselves to discuss the proper dosage, and Judy remained behind to offer Mrs. Winslow a sip of fresh water. "It won't be long now before we'll have you more comfortable," she said.

"Bless you, dear," Mrs. Winslow breathed softly. "And Dr. Belliver. Such a nice man."

"Yes, he's a very nice man," Judy agreed as she left to check the orders for the proper dose of medication. At the nurses' station, she found Wayne still perusing a chart, but George was long gone.

"Thanks, Wayne." She regarded him with a slight frown. "You're not afraid George will resent you for interfering? I would never have asked you to."

Wayne shrugged. "You didn't need to, Judy. The situation obviously needed a solution, and there's nothing I like better than finding one that satisfies everybody."

"An almost impossible task—except for you." Judy felt a flush creep up from her neck to her face, afraid that what she'd said might have sounded too personal. "Fielding can use your diplomatic skills as well as your surgical ones."

He leaned against the high counter and smiled at her. "Thanks. It's nice to have someone here that I have a history with. I'm used to working with people I've known for years, and at Fielding I scarcely know anyone. It was nice of Cliff and Angel to have me to their party the other night. I didn't see you later. Did you leave early?"

"Mmm, yes. Roger had some trouble with his back that night, poor thing. Listen, I'd better get that morphine for Mrs. Winslow after all the fuss I've made. Thanks again."

"Sure thing." He straightened and put a hand on her elbow to walk her toward the medication room. "I'd like to have had a chance to talk with Roger. He seemed like a nice guy."

"He is, but you shouldn't get the idea we're involved or anything."

He grinned. "Right. You're just friends."

"We are," Judy insisted, her expression earnest. "At least, I hope we are. Look, I've got to get that morphine. See you around, Wayne."

"See you around, Judy," he said as she slipped inside the room and allowed the door to close behind her.

Chapter Twelve

Roger had expected Judy to call him. But after the call on Saturday, arranging for her nephew to visit him, he had had no further word from her. Didn't she care that he was still in bed, and in pain, on Sunday, and Monday, and Tuesday? True, he felt a little better each day, a little more able to hobble to the bathroom or attempt to sit in a chair, but he was nowhere near ready to go back to work.

Cliff and Angel had come and put a board under his mattress. They had even met Larry, who was bringing Roger meals, which reduced the hours he owed, as well as helping Roger organize the vast quantities of medical journals lying around the house, for which he was paid. The latter project had helped Roger feel useful, since he wasn't feeling good for much. Cliff had asked Larry if he'd like to help them with their packing, so between the two "jobs," Larry was being kept off the streets and out of trouble—Roger hoped.

And the boy continued to plague him with questions about emergency medical technicians and paramedics. They found more career information on-line that Roger downloaded to a file, which he taught Larry, at a distance, to print on the printer downstairs. By Tuesday afternoon, however, Roger was restless and disturbed by Judy's defection.

When Larry arrived with his dinner, a frozen lasagna, Roger couldn't help but quiz him on what was going on at home. "Is, uh, Judy okay?"

Larry regarded him with mild irony. "Judy's always okay. Here she takes care of all these sick people, but she never comes down with anything. Not so much as a cold. You'd think working at Fielding gave her some kind of immunity."

"Hardly. So she's been working this week, has she?"

"Yeah." Larry sounded as if it was a stupid question. "She's always working. Well, maybe she doesn't work any more than Mom, but her hours are different—like weekends and things. Evenings where she doesn't get home until late. Sometimes she does double shifts when they're understaffed. That's sick, working sixteen hours in a row."

"You don't think you'd have to do that as an EMT?"

"God, I hope not." Larry frowned. "Well, maybe it

wouldn't be so bad if you really liked what you were doing."

"Don't you think Judy does?"

Impatiently, Larry brushed aside the question. "Of course she likes what she does. Otherwise she wouldn't do it."

Roger laughed. "Is that your picture of adults—that they only work at jobs they like?"

"Well, why wouldn't they? It sounds pretty stupid to me to do something you hate. Why would anyone do that?"

"Because they need the money. Because they have a family to house and feed, or because the car payment is due. A hell of a lot of people work at jobs they don't like."

"Dumb. I'm not going to."

"I hope you won't. But you shouldn't assume that other people don't have to. Do you think your mother likes her work?"

Larry shrugged. "She doesn't seem to mind it, except she was worried about being laid off. They've been doing that at the law office where she does word processing. But she could get another job."

"It's not always that simple, getting another job. And in the meantime the rent is due, the groceries have to be bought, the utilities have to be paid. Most people never get far enough ahead to save up for times when they might not have a job. The real world's a bit tougher than you imagine, Larry."

"Maybe," the boy replied, with a total lack of interest.

Roger sighed and abandoned, for the time being, his attempt to educate the boy. Maybe no middle-class teenager believed the world was tough, even one living in a city where homeless people wandered the streets. Probably kids weren't old enough or wise enough to realize that it wasn't always the "other" guy who wound up a beggar.

Teenagers thought they were invulnerable. Roger had seen that dozens of times when they came through the operating room as trauma cases. It was never going to be them who had the car accident or got shot. Not the middle-class kids, anyway. The poorer kids, the ghetto kids, knew it could very easily be them, and it went a long way toward ruining their lives.

"Is Judy working today?" Roger asked.

"Yeah, I think so. In the evening, maybe. She didn't leave until afternoon." Larry got up from the chair he'd pulled up near the bed and the laptop computer. "I got stuff to make a salad. You sure you want one?"

"I'm sure," Roger said, "with blue cheese dressing, which is in the fridge."

"Okay, you've got it."

When the boy had left him alone, Roger dialed Fielding Medical Center and asked for the nurses' station on the oncology floor. "This is Dr. Janek. Is Judy Povalski there?"

While he waited for her to come on the line, he drummed his fingers on the side of the bed. Maybe he shouldn't call her if she hadn't called him. Maybe she thought their having slept together was a mistake that couldn't be overlooked and gotten past. Why else would she not have called him?

He heard the phone click on and Judy's voice asking, "Roger? How are you?"

"Better. But still pretty much bedridden. Maybe in another day or two I'll be able to get up."

"I hope so. Is Larry behaving himself?"

"Oh, yes. He's been a big help. He hasn't got a clue about real life, has he?"

He could hear Judy's sigh. "Not really. But he'll learn. He's still young."

"I know he will. I didn't mean it as a criticism. Look, Judy, I wonder if you could do me a favor."

There was the briefest hesitation before she said, "Sure, Roger. What is it?"

He should have had a messenger service do it. There wasn't any reason he should ask her to be an errand person for him. But Roger still said, "Rachel Weis has an ethics committee report that I need to review and sign by tomorrow. I thought if you could pick it up from her and bring it over here . . ."

"I don't get off work until eleven, Roger. And you

know what it's like. I might not get out of here until almost midnight if it's a rough shift."

"That would be okay, if you came by at midnight. I'd just stay awake."

"Mmmm. Why don't you have Larry come over and pick it up? Then you can review it this evening and send it back with him tomorrow?"

Roger shifted uncomfortably on the bed. "I was kind of hoping to see you, Judy. It's very isolating being laid up this way."

"I'm sure Angel and Cliff have been there to see you, and probably Dr. Stoner, too. In fact, I'll bet Rachel would bring the report over if you asked her, on her way home."

"You don't want to come?"

Roger could almost feel the struggle she went through. "All right. I'll bring it by. Have Larry leave the key in your mailbox, okay?"

"Sure. Thanks, Judy. I appreciate it."

When he had hung up, he stared at the picture of Kerri for a long time before rolling over on his side and picking up a section of the morning's paper.

Rachel's office, ostensibly a converted closet, was full but tidy. When Judy poked her head around the door, Rachel was just gathering up her purse and several loose stacks of paper. Fielding's premier medical ethicist had graying, curly hair and sharp brown eyes. "Are you Judy?" she asked.

"Yes. I agreed to take the papers to Dr. Janek."

"I would have brought them, but it's nice of you to offer."

Judy didn't correct the woman's impression. "I'm not sure how he's going to get them back here tomorrow. Maybe my nephew will do it. He's been helping Roger out."

"So I hear." Rachel regarded her curiously. "Is that working out okay? Roger had talked with Jerry about it before he got involved."

If she hadn't been on duty, Judy would have liked to sit down and discuss the whole situation with this warm, interested woman. But she was in a hurry to return to her floor, having used her break to search out Rachel's office. "It's working better than I'd expected." She accepted the handful of papers Rachel offered her. "It sounds like Dr. Stoner has been a big help to Roger since his wife's death."

"Jerry's very good with people," Rachel admitted with a rueful smile.

"One always hopes a psychiatrist will be." Judy backed toward the door with a quick wave.

"He's always happy to talk with anyone at Fielding who needs his help," Rachel called after her.

Did she need his help? Judy wondered as she walked back up to her floor. Surely her decision to honor Roger's wish for nothing more than friendship was simple enough. She had no choice. Except maybe to have very little to do with him, which is what she supposed she'd chosen. For her own protection, obviously. It would be easy enough to become too attached to him, and he wasn't available. As she started down the corridor on her floor, she noticed that two of the call lights were on for her patients, and she hurried into the first of the two rooms.

It was after eleven-thirty when Judy arrived at Roger's house. The outside light was on, and she could see lights coming through the curtains in the living room, as well as his bedroom upstairs. The key was in the mailbox, as they had agreed upon, and she let herself in.

There was a faint odor of Italian food in the downstairs hallway, and Judy was tempted to check if Larry had cleaned up in the kitchen. Instead she climbed the staircase to the second floor, calling softly as she went so as not to startle Roger if he'd fallen asleep.

There was no answering call from him. Judy felt a momentary alarm, but forced it down, knowing how deeply sick people could sleep. The door to his bedroom was open, and she could see that he was not in bed, though the covers were pushed back and piles of books and papers rested there. "Roger!" she called sharply. "Where are you?"

A muffled cry came from the bathroom. Tossing her handful of papers on the bed, she hurried through the connecting door, to find him clinging to the edge of the stall shower, the water still pouring down on him. Judy reached in and turned off the water first, before grabbing up the bath towel he'd set out for himself. "What the hell were you trying to do?" she demanded. "You're supposed to be in bed."

"I was better. I hadn't had a spasm in two days, and I felt so grungy from lying in bed." The words came through gritted teeth. "Jesus, Judy, I can't move."

This was an exaggeration. He had propped himself in a corner of the shower, and he was stomping one foot in pain and frustration. Judy saw the cane he'd left outside the shower, but she wasn't sure it was going to be enough. Besides, he'd have to be dried off before he could get back in his bed.

"It's a good thing I'm a nurse," she grumbled as she patted his naked body down with the towel. He was not, after all, the first man whose genitals she'd seen today. But he *was* the first one she'd previously made love with, and it flustered her slightly, something that she worked hard to hide. "There. I think that's as good as I can get you while you're in there. I'm going to give you the cane for your right hand, and I'll stand on your left so you can grab me if you need to."

"I don't know if I can do it."

"You'll have to. You don't have any choice."

He moaned and gritted his teeth. "Okay. Really slowly, Judy. This is the pits."

Together they hobbled toward the bedroom, one step at a time, sometimes pausing as he drew in a sharp, pained breath. Judy kept up a steady stream of encouragement. When they reached the bed, Judy cleared away the papers, and he dropped onto it with a grimace and an escaped growl of anguish. Roger lay on his back, panting and exhausted.

"This isn't supposed to happen, you know," he said as she drew the covers over his naked body. "I'm supposed to be making steady progress toward getting back to work."

Judy smiled sympathetically. "I know. And usually it doesn't, but, hey, what's a rule if it can't be broken? I'll get you some fresh pajamas, but you may want to relax for a while before we try to get them on you."

"It was the soap," he said suddenly. "It slipped out of my hand, and I automatically grabbed for it. Made my back twist exactly wrong. Really dumb of me."

"Don't think about it." Judy walked to a bureau that looked promising and indicated the top drawer. "Are your pajamas in here?"

He flushed. "Second drawer."

Judy pulled out the drawer and found a wide selection of socks, underpants, undershirts, a few pairs of pajamas, and one filmy, feminine nightgown. Geez, the man's house was booby-trapped. She selected a pair of dark blue lightweight pajamas and closed the drawer.

"I had to keep it," Roger said, his voice low and agonized. "I gave all of her other clothes away. Angel helped me. But I had to keep the nightgown."

"You don't have to explain to me, Roger. We all keep reminders of special people." Judy set the pajamas on the bed within reach of him. "I'm not sure I should leave you here alone, when you've aggravated your back. Do you have pain medication?"

"Oh, yeah. I'll be fine," he said bravely, his brown eyes filled with appeal.

Judy snorted. "Men are such babies about being sick. I'll spend the night, Roger, but I'm exhausted. I've got to hit the sack soon."

He brightened. "That's fine. Honest. I just don't think I should be alone right now."

"I'm sure you shouldn't." But I don't think I'm the one who should be here with you, she added mentally. "What can I get you before I go to bed?"

"A fresh glass of water, if you wouldn't mind." He frowned. "I don't know how I'm going to make this up to you, Judy, but I will. I don't want you to think I wanted you to come here to be a nurse. That's not it at all. I just wanted to see you, to make sure we could be friends."

"We can be friends, Roger." Judy dropped down on the edge of the bed, regarding him seriously. "I'm not going to try to take Angel's place as your friend, though. I'm not going to be your comforter for the loss of your wife. If that's what you want from me, I can't give it. I don't want to give it."

He shifted restlessly on the bed. "That's not what I want from you."

"What do you want?"

"Someone I can be happy with. Like at the Russian River when we laughed and told stories about people at the hospital. I want to have some fun again. I'm exhausted with feeling sad and guilty."

"I'm not sure you can control those feelings." Judy felt a strong impulse to trace the lines of sorrow on his face, but kept her hands firmly in her lap. "But I know what you mean. You're ready to try to get back to normal. I hope you can. I know this has been a hard year for you. And I know you're not ready to get involved in another relationship. But you're at a different point in your life than I am."

"What point are you at?"

"I'm looking for a long-term, intimate relationship. I can be friends with you, or with any personable man, but frankly, friendship is not what I'm looking for. I have women friends, and I have my sister. And basically I find women far more rewarding as friends than men."

"Why?"

"Because we have more in common. We can talk about all kinds of things that men aren't interested in discussing—emotions, personalities, relationships.

I'm not interested in sports, and I'm not particularly interested in cars. I know very little about computers, and, as far as medicine goes, I'm much more interested in the patient than in the disease. And mostly it's women who see things the way I see them, and want to talk about them in ways I understand."

"Men talk about those things, too."

"Not much. Get a bunch of men together and they talk baseball or politics. Get a bunch of women together and they talk about the people in their lives and how they're trying to solve problems with them, at home, at work, in their activities. Those are the things that interest me. Sure, it would be fine to have a man friend to escort me to some hospital function now and then. Maybe I could even be talked into going to the theater or the symphony, because somehow it's nice to have a guy when you're doing something a little more formal."

Roger was looking rather shocked, but Judy was trying to tell him the truth. When she had stopped talking, there was a long pause. Finally, he said, "I don't understand. Are you trying to tell me you're more interested in women than men?"

Judy laughed. "No, Roger, I'm not trying to tell you I'm a lesbian. I'm as heterosexual as the next person. I'm physically attracted to men. But because men are so much more difficult to deal with psychologically than women, I prefer to only attempt that kind of intimacy in a full-blown relationship. That doesn't make any sense to you, does it?"

Roger looked worn and depressed. "No."

"Well, I'm not going to try to explain it tonight. I'm too tired, and you're in too much pain. But the bottom line is, don't count on me to take Angel's place as far as friendship goes, okay?"

"Okay."

Judy brought him a fresh glass of water and turned off the overhead light. He kept on the bedside lamp so that he could read the ethics committee report that she'd brought him. "Good night, Roger. I'll leave the doors open between our rooms. If you need something, all you have to do is call."

"Thanks, Judy. See you in the morning."

Chapter Thirteen

She slept like a rock. If he got up for any reason, she didn't hear him, and because there was no clock in her room, she had no idea what time it was when she awoke. The sun was streaming into the guest room; in fact, it had come so far into the room that it reached her head on the pillow. Judy suspected that it was quite a bit after her usual time to get up, but since she didn't have to be at work until mid-afternoon, she wasn't particularly alarmed.

Then it occurred to her that poor Roger was probably starving, and she jumped out of bed wearing the T-shirt she'd swiped from his underwear drawer. No reason to wrinkle her own clothes by sleeping in them. She could see that he was lying in bed, holding papers up so that he could read them from a recumbent position. "What time is it?" she called across.

Roger glanced at his bedside clock and said, "Quarter to ten."

"Wow! I'm sorry. I'll get you something to eat in just a minute. How's your back?"

"Not as bad as I thought it would be, but not as good as yesterday morning, either."

Judy had taken herself out of his line of vision to don her clothes. She caught a glimpse of herself in a small mirror on the wall and tried to tame her disheveled hair by running her fingers through it. She'd left her purse with a comb in Roger's bedroom. Well, what could he expect, asking her to spend the night on such short notice? He'd just have to take her as she was.

From his doorway she offered to make him something special—pancakes or waffles if he'd like and if he had the proper ingredients downstairs. But Roger assured her that a bowl of cereal and a peach would be fine. It seemed to Judy that he wasn't quite meeting her eyes, that he was withdrawn or embarrassed. With a mental shrug she left him to see what his kitchen had in the way of cereal and fruit. With any luck her nephew would have replenished supplies as they diminished. But Judy wasn't sure Larry understood that concept.

In the kitchen she found a counter full of boxes and plates, as though Larry hadn't bothered to put them away because he was just going to use them again. An interesting accommodation. There were two boxes of cereal, and she decided to choose for Roger since he'd no doubt told Larry what cereals he liked. The bowls, too, were on the blue-tile countertop, as well as spoons and forks and knives. Well, maybe it wasn't such a bad idea, if no one else was going to be around the kitchen, to leave everything out this way. It certainly saved a lot of work.

Of course, Judy found last night's dishes in the sink, soaking in a plastic tub of once soapy water. Not a perfect solution, she thought, but at Roger's house, Larry was Roger's problem. And Roger would probably never know about the dirty dishes. Not that Judy intended to do them. She'd do the ones she created and leave the others for Larry when he returned.

A large tray was laid out with a glass and a napkin, all ready to go upstairs. From the window Judy could see roses growing in the backyard. On impulse she found a pair of scissors and went out to cut three flowers of different colors—red, orange, and yellow—to put on Roger's tray in a teardrop-shaped bud vase she found in a high cabinet. He deserved a little cheering up.

After she'd poured two bowls of cereal and a pitcher of milk, found a peach in the refrigerator and sugar on the counter, she carried the laden tray upstairs. Roger took one look at the bud vase with its colorful roses and grimaced.

"I used to do that for Kerri," he said. "She loved the flowers, especially the yellow roses."

"Eat your cereal, Roger."

Yes, Judy decided, she definitely wasn't interested in being "just friends" with him. The memory of Kerri, the continual referral to her name, put a distinct distance between her and Roger, one which she suspected he unconsciously wished to have there. And even though the wish might have been unconscious, it was very powerful. Nobody was going to come between him and his memories of his dead wife. He could talk all he wanted to about having fun again; he wasn't ready.

They discussed the ethics committee report as they ate their cereal, and when they were finished Judy gathered the dishes together and returned them downstairs. She washed only the ones she and Roger had used, determined to make Larry do his share of the work. He was, after all, being paid for his efforts.

Before leaving the house, she collected the signed report, set out food, water, medicine, books, and the phone for Roger. He watched her with a wary expression and finally asked, "Aren't you going to tell me more about what you were saying last night?"

"No, I don't think so. I pretty much covered what I had to say."

"Where does that leave us?"

"As casual friends. I'm not going to be coming by, or calling you. I'm not going to hold your hand. I don't feel comfortable in that kind of relationship. If I'm going to hold someone's hand, it will be for a stranger, a patient who doesn't ask for the same kind of emotional involvement."

"But Angel and Cliff are leaving in a few days. And I'm stranded here."

"Hardly stranded, Roger. Larry will be coming by. Jerry Stoner and Rachel Weis would be happy to help you. Besides, your back is going to feel fine in another few days."

Even to herself she sounded callous. Roger looked positively unbelieving that she could so summarily dismiss him. "It won't be the same," he said. "I'll miss seeing you."

"Not that much. You'll be busy getting well, and I'll be busy at work. When you come back to Fielding, we'll see each other around the hospital."

"Would you go to the theater with me sometime when I'm well?"

"Probably not." She smiled to take the sting from the words. "There are lots of people who'd like to take care of you, Roger. I'm just not one of them."

"But we slept together."

Judy shrugged. "So we made a mistake. I'm not going to cry over it. I'm just going to get on with my life."

Roger looked torn, but he said nothing, his fingers picking nervously at the newspaper that lay beside him on the bed. "Well, thanks for helping me. Tell

Rachel I think the report is great. Maybe she could give me a call."

"I'll tell her." Judy stood in the doorway and blew him a farewell kiss. "Take care of yourself, Roger."

"Sure."

He looked confused, and a little lost. Judy had to steel herself to actually turn away from him. But her own peace of mind was important. She had a demanding job and a stressful living situation with her sister and nephew. One more demand, of this magnitude, and she wouldn't be able to concentrate on her work. If she allowed herself to get more involved with Roger, who was not ready to cope with his side of an emotional involvement, she would simply be hurting herself.

As she hurried down the stairs and out of the house, she considered the outsider's view that many nurses were codependent. Well, this one wasn't. She knew how to protect herself, and in this case that meant walking away from the situation. Funny that people thought of nurses that way. No one considered physicians codependent, and they professed to be as eager to help patients as nurses were. Nurses, on the other hand, did the dirty work. Was there something demeaning about that? Was there something inherently dishonorable about doing for patients what they were physically unable to do for themselves? Judy didn't believe that for a minute.

But staying to take care of Roger would have been

a different matter. They weren't talking about taking care of his body, they were talking about taking care of his spirit. Roger wanted her to stay and be available while he continued to heal from his wife's death. In return she would get a grateful man, who was dependent on her in an unhealthy way. Not a good solution, for either of them, even if he didn't understand that now.

Later, when she returned to the hospital for her evening shift, she dropped by Rachel's office with the ethics committee report. Rachel already had a visitor in her small office. Jerry Stoner, the psychiatrist with whom she was living, was sitting across the desk from her, and Judy hesitated at the door.

"Knock, knock," she said, looking questioningly at them.

"Come in," Rachel urged. "You know Jerry."

"Hi, Dr. Stoner. Thanks for helping Roger make a decision about my nephew. Roger hasn't given up on him yet, and my sister and I think Larry's coming along a bit."

"I think he'll do just fine, from everything Roger's told me. Compared with the kids I hear about who *really* get in trouble, your nephew's practically a saint. Roger's been good for him, and I think probably he's been good for Roger."

Judy nodded thoughtfully. "I think so, too."

"Good. How's Roger's back?"

"Not so great. He accidentally strained it again."

The two of them looked at her curiously, and she shook her head and laughed. "He was grabbing for a bar of soap in the shower. Honest." She produced the manila envelope and handed it to Rachel. "He said to tell you he thinks the report is great."

"Good. It was a help having him on the committee."

"I think," Judy added, including both of them in her professionally concerned gaze, "that Roger is worried about Cliff and Angel leaving. I'm going to be very busy for a while, so I won't be able to fill in. Maybe the two of you could?"

Looking perplexed, but accommodating, Rachel said, "Well, sure we will. Does he have some help during the day?"

"He's paying Larry, my nephew, to bring in meals and things. It's the emotional support he needs."

Jerry, his hair grown a little longer than she remembered, cocked his head inquisitively. "Are you going on vacation?"

"No, I've just got a full schedule, with work and trying to learn about computers, and my nephew and everything. I don't really know Roger all that well. There was this thing with my nephew, of course, but before that I'd hardly spoken with him. So I'm not really the kind of long-term friend he needs to stand by him now."

"I see."

Jerry actually looked like he did indeed understand. Psychiatrists often did, Judy supposed. "Well, I'll be off. I've got to be on the floor in five minutes. Thanks."

"Thank *you*," Rachel said, but little worry lines had appeared between her eyes.

"Discretion is almost always the better part of valor," Jerry murmured as Judy let herself out the door.

Roger was back on his feet for part of the day by the time Cliff and Angel were leaving for Wisconsin. They drove over to his house in their car loaded down with suitcases and medical paraphernalia that they weren't prepared to trust to the moving company. It was early Saturday morning, a week after their party, and the July day promised to be clear and sunny.

From his location in the driver's seat, Cliff said, "We aren't coming in. If I let Angel into your house, she'll start to organize your whole life, trust me."

Angel, who looked about to deliver her baby any minute, even though she was only eight months pregnant, wrinkled her nose at him. "He's just annoyed because he knows how many pit stops we're going to have to make on our way across country. I'll probably see the inside of every other restroom in five states."

Cliff groaned and climbed out of the car to shake hands with Roger. "We're going to miss you, Roger.

Hope you won't regret selling the cottage, but with Jerry already having an empty house, and Angel and I going back to Wisconsin, it seemed a good time."

"Oh, I agree. It was time to get rid of it." He turned to Angel who had gotten out and come around the car to put her arm around his waist. "And thanks for packing up all my personal things from the cabin, Angel. I've just left the boxes in the garage, but someday I'll look through them."

"I know you will. There are some books you'll want in the house. I guess you'd already brought back all the pictures."

"Yeah, once when I was up with Jerry."

Cliff had been eyeing the house in a curious fashion and now asked, "Where's Judy? I'd hoped to get a chance to say good-bye to her."

"Oh, she's decided not to hang around," Roger said in a falsely casual tone.

"What?" Angel tightened her arm around his waist. "But I thought you were becoming good friends."

"She didn't want to be friends."

Angel gave a tsk of annoyance. "Why didn't you tell us, Roger? What are you going to do?"

"Hey, I'm perfectly all right," Roger protested. "But I'll miss you guys."

"We'll miss you, too," Cliff assured him, but the firm warning in his voice was for his wife. "We have to get on the road, Angel. Jerry and Rachel are around. Nan and Steve are around. We're history."

"Thanks for everything you've done." Roger hugged Angel and gave her a sweet kiss. "Call me and let me know how things are going. Hope the baby pops right out."

Angel grinned. "Me, too."

Roger watched as they climbed back in the car and pulled quickly away from the curb, waving until their car turned the corner. He wished they could have stayed a little longer. He wished they hadn't left before the anniversary of his wedding almost a year ago, and the date of Kerri's death a few weeks later. Jerry and Rachel were good friends, but it wasn't the same. Nan and Steve were on vacation and wouldn't be back until after the sad occasion. Roger felt very much alone.

Judy saw both Roger and Wayne in the hospital during the following weeks. She was friendly toward both of them, and kept a clear distance, a professional distance. Because on every front in her personal and professional life, Judy found herself struggling, as she often had, with the need to be valued, to be recognized for herself.

There was no way she was going to put herself in a situation of being ministering angel to Roger, when their one sexual encounter had convinced her she had more than a platonic friendship in mind. They had to deal with each other as emotional equals, or not at all.

During her relationship with Wayne, she had realized something important about herself. Only in that kind of physical, intimate relationship did she feel accepted on an even footing with the men in her life. In the OR she certainly hadn't been, even by the best of the doctors. There, she had had to accept her subordinate role, because she was a nurse, without the training and knowledge of a physician.

Most nurses were women, and their work was considered peripheral, undemanding, and subservient. Because of this, Judy was regarded as not as intelligent, not as professional, and not as worthy as those on the rungs above her in the hospital hierarchy. Doctors tended to depreciate her achievements as a nurse, and, more subtly, as a woman.

With Wayne it had been different. He had talked with her outside the OR and learned who she was, what she liked, where she'd come from. Even before they became involved, she had felt he understood what her job required, and that she was not just a cipher.

Coming out of her affair with Wayne had been a double torture for her. Not only had she lost that intimate relationship where she had felt a personal equal, but her work life had been affected as well. In the OR he was kind to her, considerate, but he treated her differently than he had when they were lovers. Naturally, that happened when someone fell out of love with you, but it had left her feeling unsure of her importance as both a nurse and a woman.

It had taken considerable time and effort to achieve a new balance in her life. And even that had been undermined at home by her nephew, with his teenage dismissal of both Judy and Liza. It had not helped Judy's self-esteem, either, to watch as Roger, his back restored to its normal functioning, drew Larry into his life, and made real progress in turning her nephew into a more considerate human being.

So this was a time when Judy needed to feel as capable and appreciated as possible. Keeping Roger and Wayne at arm's length was useful, but hardly a solution. And in mid-July George Carruthers, the surgical resident she'd had a run-in with a few weeks previously, became more demanding and less patient each time he and Judy had a problem.

"Anyone can hold a patient's hand!" he snapped one day. "Anyone can wipe a patient's butt. Anyone can start an IV and give medications. What's the big deal, Judy? I have twice as many patients as you do to be responsible for—their lives are in my hands. And you can't manage to get someone his lunch on time!"

He had chosen the most public spot possible, in front of the nursing station, for this confrontation. A momentary pause in the doctors' and nurses' conversations occurred, before they hurriedly restarted. Judy considered making an angry reply. She even, despairingly, contemplated the hazards of walking off the floor and not returning. He wouldn't have spoken that way to another doctor, no matter how furious he was with him, or even her.

Judy raised her brows a fraction. "Are you asking me why Mr. Lee doesn't have his lunch tray, Doctor?"

"No, I'm telling you to get your butt in gear and get it in there. It's one-thirty."

"Because if you want to know why Mr. Lee doesn't have his lunch tray, it's because he was asleep when I offered to bring it at twelve-thirty and his wife said she'd ring when he was ready. She hasn't rung."

George's face flushed with anger. Between gritted teeth he said, "He's in there screaming that he wants his lunch, Judy. He says he's asked five times."

"Mr. Lee also has Alzheimer's, Doctor. He's not always clear on time sequences. His wife helps him manage, and she may have gone out for a cigarette break."

"Maybe people who smoke should be shot."

Everyone in the vicinity turned to see who had made such an outrageous remark. Wayne, grinning wickedly, lounged in the door of a patient's room across the corridor from the nursing station. "Don't you think so, George?"

"No, I don't think so, Dr. Belliver," George muttered. "Though they might as well be, for the damage they do themselves."

"And others," someone chimed in, making George Carruthers look more at ease.

"Interesting viewpoint, Wayne," one of the attending surgeons remarked. His eyes glittered with amusement, but he was shaking his head. "You're going to give Fielding a bad reputation."

Judy had used the interruption to escape into the service room where food trays were kept before being zapped in the microwave. She could hear the doctors still joking out in the hallway, but she paid no attention. George's attitude and language had thoroughly distressed her.

To be treated like a recalcitrant, incompetent child by a second-year resident who knew diddly squat about surgery, nurses, or patients was almost more than she could tolerate. And the jerk had purposely done it in front of as many people as possible. Plus, he was going to be really pissed that she'd had a reasonable answer for him. He was going to be waiting for her smallest misdeed, so he could prove his superiority.

And then there was Wayne, coming to her rescue again like the cavalry. Not that it had been so apparent this time. Still, Judy decided it was time for a vacation and the chance to get back a little perspective. But her head nurse said it was summer, for God's sake, and what was Judy thinking of?

Chapter Fourteen

As the first anniversary of his wedding day approached, Roger became more agitated. Already he was trying to keep himself busy every minute of the day. When he wasn't at work, he was catching up on journal reading, or renting videos that would require his whole attention. With Larry he worked on the computer, gave tennis lessons, even arranged with Steve's help an expedition for the two of them on an ambulance. But Roger missed having Angel to call, and he missed Cliff's bracing insistence that he get on with his life.

Roger was trying to get on with his life. He was experiencing a curious mixture of hope and despair. Mornings he sometimes awoke with a feeling of rejuvenation, as if it were spring and he was some plant that had new life coursing through its veins. He felt right on the verge of happiness, the nibblings of a joyful expectation. And when he remembered Kerri, when his mind insisted that he deal with the fact that she was dead and gone from the world, he felt a sadness that was largely for her.

For most of the past year he had felt sorry for himself, that he had lost her, that he wouldn't get to spend his life with her. Now he thought how sad it was that she had died so young, without the opportunity to experience a real marriage or children or any of the myriad things living into your sixties and seventies and longer allowed. Roger even thought, on some of the bright mornings, how sad it was that she wasn't there to experience the day itself with its summer sun and fog and whispering breezes.

But the farther away he got from her actual presence, the harder it was for him to remember exactly what it was they'd said to each other, what they'd anticipated their lives would be like before her relapse. He knew she had been perfect and filled with beauty. He knew he had been very lucky to find her, and that she had loved him. But the vast hole that had existed in him at her death, like a deep wound, was healing.

His anniversary fell on a Saturday. Roger would have preferred that it had fallen on a weekday, when at least the majority of his time would have been taken up by work. Instead he woke at eight to an overcast, cool summer day. He had arranged to give Larry a tennis lesson in Golden Gate Park at three, hoping that would distract him from an acute awareness of what day it was. Still, a long day stretched in front of him.

Over a hearty breakfast of eggs and bacon, toast and coffee, he tried to concentrate on the newspaper. The headlines were uninteresting, and only two or three of the stories truly captured his attention. What he didn't realize for a while was that he was trying to ignore a deep knowledge in himself that today was a very important day, and not in the way he had pretended. Today was the day, if he was strong enough, that he was going to close a few doors into the past.

When he had finished the breakfast dishes, he returned to his bedroom and opened the drawer where he kept not only his pajamas, but the special nightgown of Kerri's, the one piece of clothing that he'd kept when she had died. He ran his hands over the silky fabric for the last time, then gently wrapped it in tissue paper and folded it into a large manila envelope. He couldn't bear letting anyone else have it, and he hated to destroy it, but he needed to have it out of his house. On the way to the park he would find a refuse can and leave it there, like any other discard from his life.

Then he went downstairs to the garage, where the Audi was looking a little more presentable since he and Larry were working on it together. In the recesses under the back of the house were the boxes that Angel had packed at the cabin, filled with personal things from his room there. He dragged the boxes into a better lit section of the garage and started going through the contents.

There were books and some forgotten clothes, but only his. If there had been any of Kerri's there, Angel had already removed them. There was a funny little bean-filled figure that Kerri had used as a paperweight, and a scarf she'd worn to freezing night games at Candlestick Park. Probably, Angel had thought it was his. Roger sorted everything into two piles—one to be kept and distributed upstairs among his other things, and one to be given away to Goodwill.

Many of the books were Kerri's, ones she had used in her teaching. Because he wanted to take care of everything today, Roger decided he would simply leave a box of them on the doorstep of the local middle school. If they didn't want them, they could give them away, but Kerri would have liked the idea of their being available to the kids. She would have liked, too, what he was doing with Larry, he thought, though he had been less than completely successful. Kerri would not have expected miracles. She hadn't even expected one for herself.

It took him several hours to sort through everything, to distribute what he was keeping upstairs among his other possessions, and to prepare the rest to be disposed of. After a sandwich for lunch, he returned once again to his bedroom and took the wedding album Angel had made for them from the shelf. It had gathered dust while he was away, living in Nan's flat, and he obviously hadn't had it down since. In the house, there were six different pictures of Kerri alone or Kerri with him.

Roger forced himself to pick his favorite, the two of them on a friend's sailboat when Kerri had been healthy. The rest of the pictures he removed from their frames and put in the album with the wedding pictures. They would always be there for him to look at, but they would be contained in a more restricted space. He didn't need more in the house, because Kerri was a part of him, and always would be.

Roger realized he didn't have to be afraid that she would disappear from his heart just because he went on with life. She wasn't the whole of his heart anymore, but that didn't matter. She was his special memory, the loving spirit in his past. That wouldn't change if he put away the pictures of her, or gave away her books. But he had to keep the house from becoming a museum dedicated to her, and he had to keep himself from being the docent who described her meaning to the world.

He dropped off the boxes at the school and a Goodwill truck before he stopped to pick up Larry. The manila envelope still sat on the passenger seat. He had passed two debris boxes and several refuse cans, but it was hard to dispose of this last me-

mento. Because he'd given himself plenty of time to take care of his errands, he was fifteen minutes early arriving at Larry's. When he pulled up to the curb, he saw the teenage boy hard at work on Judy's Honda, his hands black with grease, a triumphant smile on his lips.

Judy herself stood there in blue jeans and a plaid flannel shirt, apparently mocking him for his disgustingly dirty shirt and hands. Neither of them had seen Roger yet, and he sat still in the driver's seat watching as they laughed and Larry reached over to draw a greasy finger down his aunt's cheek. She made a mock feint at him, still laughing, and then climbed into the car to try starting it. He heard the rough roar of the engine and saw Larry's double thumbs-up sign. Just at that moment Larry saw him, too, and waved.

"You're early," he called as he snapped down the lid of the green tool box at his feet. "Let me change my shirt and wash my hands, and I'll be right with you."

Roger had climbed out of the car and called, "Take your time," to the departing boy. Judy hadn't moved from her position inside the Civic, so Roger walked over and bent down to say hello. Judy acknowledged him warily. "I'm here to take Larry for a tennis lesson," he explained.

"I knew you were coming, but I thought it was later." She turned off the engine and rubbed ineffectually at the grease streak on her cheek. "Larry's getting pretty good at this car-repair stuff, but he seems to think everyone should get filthy doing it."

"Come and look at the Audi. He's hammered out the worst of the dent, used some of that body putty, and sprayed paint on to disguise the damage. No one would ever take it for brand-new, but it doesn't look bad."

Roger held the door open for her, and she followed him to the curb, where she whistled appreciatively at his car. "Not bad at all. If he doesn't make it as a paramedic, he can always do car repair. That was great, your giving him a chance to ride on the ambulance, Roger. You never heard a kid talk so long about such a short period of time."

Roger grinned. "He talked just as much to me about it, and I was there at the time."

"Well, I think the interest is all to the good. When school starts in the fall, he'll have a goal to work toward. Liza and I really appreciate what you've done, Roger. She was talking a while back about an appropriate way to thank you."

"Tell her not to bother." Roger scratched his ear, one of his old nervous habits. "He's no paragon of virtue yet. He's almost never on time, and he didn't tell me the truth about getting Liza's permission to go sailing with a group of us."

Judy frowned. "He lied to you?"

"Well, he said it was okay with her, but I checked

and he hadn't actually asked. Larry told me he didn't have to because Liza approved of everything we did together."

"I suppose that's pretty much true, but he should have asked if you told him to."

"We agreed to add ten hours to his service time as a consequence. Does that sound fair?"

Judy snorted. "Hell, at this rate, Roger, you'll have him in your hair forever. I'm not sure spending time with you serves as much of a punishment."

"I make him work, too. We don't just go off and do fun things like playing tennis. But I enjoy spending time with him, Judy. I'll feel a little lost when he finishes up his obligation, and that's not going to take long now. He'll be done before school starts."

"Then you'll see if he wants to spend time with you just because it's fun or because he has to. I'd be surprised if he didn't want to hang around."

"But kids get busy when school starts. He won't need the diversion so much then."

Judy's gaze seemed to rest on the manila envelope, though Roger could think of no reason she should suspect what was in it. She stepped back from the car and said, "We'll just have to wait and see. I'm betting he'll want to spend time with you."

"I hope so." He wanted to say something personal to her, but how could he? He couldn't very well remind her of the night they'd spent together, or that she hadn't been willing to stand by him when he'd needed her to. "Are you taking a vacation this summer?" he asked finally.

Judy grimaced. "I was hoping to get away this coming week, but apparently they can't manage without me. I really feel burned-out, though, and it's not great working when you don't feel on top of things."

"How come you're feeling burned-out?"

"Lots of stuff. Nothing I could explain, exactly. I just feel like I need a break."

"Where would you go?"

She shrugged. "Santa Barbara, maybe, where I have a friend. Or maybe I'd drive to Seattle and stay with another friend there. That would be a nice change of pace. I enjoy Seattle."

"These friends," Roger said, "are they women friends?"

"Yes. Why?"

"Oh, I was just curious. You know, you said you just like to be friends with women."

"It works better that way, yes. These are women I met in college, or when I was nursing; people who have moved away. Lots of them have stayed at my apartment over the years, so I've got good credits built up. It's great to visit them and catch up on their lives, and have a chance to explore their cities while they're at work. With the nurses you can exchange war stories, which is a good way of blowing off steam. So I usually come back feeling better."

"Didn't you come back after our time in the Russian River feeling better?"

"Well, sure, but that wasn't the same."

"Why not?"

Judy regarded him suspiciously. "Roger, I don't understand what you're getting at."

Feeling that he'd upset her, he said, "Nothing. Just that you and I could be friends, too. That it would be rewarding."

"We *are* friends. We're just nothing more than friends, and we're not very close friends. That's the best way for it to be, Roger."

If Larry hadn't stormed down the stairs then, Roger might have argued with her. But the boy burst through the front door, his tennis racket swinging aggressively in his right hand. "I'm ready, Roger," he called. "Bet I can beat you today."

"Really?" Judy asked, surprised.

"No, he's just a cocky little kid. He's got a long way to go yet." Roger rumpled the boy's hair, something Larry didn't much appreciate but tolerated. Then he tossed the teenager his keys, at the same time saying to Judy, "I'm also trying to improve his driving skills."

"You?"

"Yes, me. I can drive really well when I concentrate on it."

Judy looked skeptical, and Roger remembered that his driving was how this whole thing got started—the thing with her nephew, he added mentally. There was no *thing* between him and Judy. He climbed into the Audi, laying the manila envelope on his lap. Larry started the car and pulled cautiously away from the curb. Judy waved briefly at them and turned away, her attention immediately transferred back to her car.

Roger played a really energetic game of tennis, calling on all of Larry's competitive instincts to make it challenging. Though he won handily, he could tell that the boy was delighted with his own progress, and with being treated as though he were a worthy opponent. On their way back to the car, Roger shoved the manila envelope way down into a trash can and walked away without looking back.

"How about a hamburger?" he asked.

"Sure. I told Mom we might get something." Larry, a cheerful opportunist, suggested that they go to Bill's instead of McDonald's.

"You're on."

Shortly after Roger returned home, the phone rang. He answered it as he snapped on the table lamp that glowed on the one picture of Kerri that remained in the den. Angel's voice floated into the room with him.

"Hi, Roger. I've been thinking about you today, remembering the wedding in the hospital and how lovely Kerri looked. And how proud you were. I hope you haven't been alone all day."

"No, I spent the afternoon playing tennis with Larry, and then we had a hamburger at Bill's. And I did a lot of cleaning out today, it just seemed the right time. She was beautiful that day, wasn't she? I'm so glad she agreed to marry me."

"So am I. That's what she wanted. You made her very happy, Roger."

"Did I? It's hard to remember that now." He dropped down onto the leather chair, still staring at the photograph. "How are you feeling, Angel?"

"Great, now. I had the baby today."

"Today? You did? Jesus, why didn't you say?" He was out of the chair again, suddenly alive with energy. "You're okay? The baby's okay? Cliff's okay?"

"Everyone's fine." Her voice sounded full of laughter. "It's a boy, nine pounds, fifteen ounces."

"I'm not surprised he's that size!" Roger wound the telephone cord around his fingers. "Oh, Angel, that's great. How was the labor?"

"Best forgotten. You better believe I'll be a little more sympathetic toward birthing women from now on. But it was okay, and only lasted six hours."

"Not bad. At the University Hospital?"

"Yes, with Cliff in attendance. He's not sure if it will be possible to talk me into another one just yet, but he's really tickled with his son."

"I'll bet. What are you naming him?"

"I'll put Cliff on."

There was a moment's pause before Cliff's voice boomed over the line. "I'm a father, Roger. Imagine that!"

"Congratulations, Cliff. I'm really thrilled for the two of you. Wish I could be there to see him."

"Angel was amazing. Do you have any idea how painful childbirth is?"

"Fortunately, I can only guess." Roger tried again. "Have you named him?"

"Yep. We're calling him Roger Crawford Lenzini."

It took a moment for the name to sink in. "After me? Really?" Roger's eyes flooded with tears. Through the catch in his throat, he said, "You guys are great. Will you send me a picture of him right away? Do I get to be like his godfather, or his honorary uncle?"

"Whatever you like." Cliff's own voice turned gruff. "We want you to have happy memories of today, Rog. This kid's going to be partly your responsibility. We'll expect you to teach him how to wreck cars and fish and windsurf. All those good things. Angel and I are just going to indoctrinate him in being a super kid."

"And you'll do a great job." Roger smiled to himself, thinking of how hard Angel had worked to get Cliff to understand his own male chauvinism. "I'll send him a doll, shall I?"

"Don't you dare! But don't tell Angel I said so."

He could hear them bickering in the background

and thought how they still seemed to enjoy each other, even just hours after going through childbirth together. Dear Angel, she was always willing to accommodate her surgeon husband, but she was a determined woman: Roger had no doubt that she'd manage to raise little Roger so he valued women as much as men.

As a family-practice doctor she'd need all the skill she possessed in dealing with families in her native Wisconsin. And Roger didn't doubt she'd learn a lot from them about raising kids. Roger himself was glad he was getting this experience with Larry. What could be better when little Roger came to that age?

"Let me talk to Angel before we hang up, Cliff."

Angel's voice was full of tender happiness. "So what do you think, Roger? Is it okay with you if we give our boy your name?"

"I'm really pleased, Angel. Thanks for thinking of it."

Angel laughed. "How do you know it wasn't Cliff?"

"Because it would never occur to him. But I'm glad he agreed. You've managed to make it a wonderful day after all. I miss you. But your being gone has shown me how reliant I'd become on the two of you to hold me together emotionally."

"Hardly that, Roger. We just formed a good support network. And we're still here to do that. All you have to do is call."

"Thanks. But you'll be busy, and it's time I managed to do my own supporting. Today I went through the stuff from the cottage and put away all but one picture of Kerri."

Her voice came across as warm as a hug. "That was brave of you. And wise. You don't have to forget her to get on with your life."

"I know. I didn't quite understand that for a while."

"Is everything else going okay?"

"Like work? Sure. And my back's completely healed."

"But you haven't seen any more of Judy?"

Roger's shrug was of course invisible to his friend. "I see her at Fielding sometimes, and I saw her today when I picked up Larry. That's all."

"I see."

"Well, it was her decision," he protested, as though she'd criticized his action. "She didn't want to just be friends."

"I don't blame her. But it sounds suspiciously like you do, Roger, and I don't think that's particularly fair."

"She said she'd rather have women friends."

"Did she?" Angel laughed. "I like her style. Say hello from me when you see her again."

"Okay." Roger wasn't going to argue with her about Judy. That was something she just didn't understand, obviously. "Look, I should let you go. You must be exhausted. Give my love to the baby, to Roger."

"I will. And ours to you."

After Roger had hung up, he wandered around the house thinking about the new life that had come into the world. Kerri would have been so delighted for Angel. Only then did it occur to Roger that when Kerri had died, Cliff and Angel weren't even really a couple yet, certainly not married. So very much had happened during this year, things Kerri would never know about. Death was not only final, but it seemed suddenly strange to Roger in the way time stood still for the dead.

Such a short time ago, really, a year. On his wedding day Jerry had still been an associate professor, Nan and Steve had probably not even met. The changes in ethics consults hadn't yet been considered. He and Cliff and Jerry had still owned the cottage, with no thought that they would ever sell it. All changed.

Roger knew that he had changed, too, but perhaps not as much as he would have thought a few months ago. He had learned from his trip to the Russian River with Judy that he still possessed the need to laugh and enjoy himself. He also knew from the night he'd spent with Judy here in his house that his sexual self had revived. If two-thirds of himself had recovered, the other third could not be far behind. Which frightened him, because even though he'd told Angel he'd learned that he wouldn't forget Kerri, he was not really so sure.

What if he fell in love again? Was that possible? Surely not. Kerri was the one great love of his life. If he loved again, it would be a lesser love, a plebeian love, something that anyone could have. It would be all sex, or all lightness and fluff. Because no one was like Kerri. No one. She could not be replaced. No one could ever slip into that spot in his heart.

It wouldn't be fair to Kerri.

Chapter Fifteen

The day shifts were exhausting, even though Judy preferred them to evening. There was a constant stream of doctors on the floor, with consequent orders in patient charts. There were visitors who sought information. There were always the patients, sick and often helpless, to say nothing of frightened. Most days Judy could squeeze some satisfaction from her work. But not every day.

On a Wednesday when she had an extra patient to be responsible for, and three of her patients were nearing the end of their lives, she was nearly rushed off her feet. George Carruthers continued to snipe at her, but she avoided a confrontation with him. Wayne crossed her path just often enough for her to become comfortable with him. But this Wednesday he told her that his fiancé had broken off their engagement, and she hardly knew what to say, except how sorry she was.

Wayne, like Roger, acted as though he expected some consolation from her, but she was having none of it. She was not nurse to the world. Judy was convinced that you could give and give only if you took care of yourself. And taking care of yourself meant that you didn't involve yourself in hopeless situations that were bound to break your heart.

When she got home from work, Judy literally fell onto the couch and kicked off her shoes. Liza, who had heard her come in, appeared in the living room door to say, "I'm going out with Phil tonight, Judy, and I'm worried. Larry is getting a little weird about my dating Phil. We took him out to dinner with us the other night, and he hardly said a word. When I asked him to be more friendly next time, he said there would be no next time."

Liza wandered farther into the room and dropped onto a chair with a sigh. "First time I've been interested in someone since Bob died, and Larry refuses to see him. What worries me is that it may be because of Roger, you know?"

"In what way? Roger would never interfere in something like that."

"No, I mean that Larry's gotten fond of Roger, whether he realizes it or not, and Roger's interested in him. Phil doesn't know a thing about teenagers, and he needs time to figure out how to deal with

Larry." Liza ducked her head and shifted her shoulders, her natural prelude to asking a big favor of her sister. "Do you think you could get Roger to stop seeing Larry for a while? Not forever. Just until he and Phil have a chance to work on their relationship."

"That wouldn't be fair to Roger, Liza. He said just the other day that he was worried Larry wouldn't want to see him after his hours were put in. And I was assuring him that Larry enjoyed spending time with him whether he had to or not."

"But this is important to me, Judy. I think things are going somewhere with Phil. I'm really attracted to him, and he seems to care about me."

Judy realized from Liza's earnestness that she had given the matter some thought, and had decided that this was the logical solution. To Judy it seemed that getting Larry to accept one man wasn't going to be accomplished by denying him access to someone he already enjoyed spending time with. She frowned. "You could talk with Roger about it, Liza. I suppose he might understand."

"Me talk with him? You've got to be kidding. He's your friend, Judy. He'll listen to you. And you only have to tell him we'd interrupt the community service hours for a month or two, until he gets used to Phil."

Because her day had been so exhausting, and because she knew how much Roger enjoyed working with Larry, Judy couldn't decide if this was a reasonable request.

Liza leaned forward, her eyes pleading. "Phil is a nice guy, Judy. He's willing to spend time with Larry to get things sorted out. But I don't think Larry will be willing to do it if he can see Roger instead."

"Roger has done a really good job with Larry, Liza. It just seems so ungrateful to dismiss him like this."

"We wouldn't be dismissing him," Liza insisted. "Just asking him to back off for a while."

Judy's head had begun to ache. "I know, but it sounds so unfair. We needed help with Larry, and Roger gave it. Now it would be like saying, 'Well, thanks, but we're going to replace you with someone else.' Don't you think that if Phil becomes a permanent part of your life, Larry will come to accept him without our having to disrupt a relationship he and Roger have both come to enjoy?"

Liza studied her clenched hands for a long moment. "The thing is, Judy, Phil isn't very good with Larry. Oh, he means to be! But he treats him like he's younger, you know, or tries to be all buddy-buddy with him. Larry just hates it! You can just see him comparing Phil with Roger. And, Judy, I want so much for this to work. Phil is very special to me. I wouldn't ask you if this wasn't really, really important."

Ah, the wonders of falling in love, Judy thought dispiritedly. "All right. I'll talk with Roger."

"Thank you. I really appreciate it." Liza reached over and squeezed her sister's hand. "I know you'll tell Roger how grateful we are for his help." Liza rose and moved toward the door, where she paused. "If you're going to be home, I don't think I'll be back tonight. If that's okay?"

"Sure. I'll be here. And have a good time, Liza."

Too tired to consider the problem further, Judy fell asleep on the couch. Several hours later she was startled awake by raucous laughter coming from the kitchen. It was male laughter, and she thought one of the voices was that of her nephew. Her head felt fuzzy from the unintended nap, and she sat up feeling dazed and headachy. "Larry?" she called. And there was a sudden and ominous silence from the kitchen.

Judy swung her feet down onto the floor and sat up, blinking in the weak light. It was hard to tell what time it was because the blinds had been drawn when she came in. It could have been seven or ten. "Larry?" she called again.

This time there was movement in the kitchen, the scraping of chairs, the hurried whispering of male voices. Judy began to feel a little alarmed. After another minute or two she heard stealthy footsteps going down the stairs toward the outside and the thump of the kitchen window thrown open. What the hell was going on?

Next the refrigerator door opened and, after a moment, closed. Then a cabinet clicked open and shut. Soon water ran in the sink, and there was the clash of dishes against the enamel surface. Surely, no burglar in history had done the dishes before disappearing. Judy rose to her stocking feet and marched out into the hall, pausing only briefly at the kitchen door before entering that well-lit room.

Larry stood at the sink, hurriedly rinsing plates and glasses in a sink full of sudsy water. He looked up with feigned innocence from his task and said, "Oh, hi, Judy. I didn't know you were home. There weren't any lights on when I got in."

The clock on the stove said it was 9:47. Outside the light was mostly gone. There was a suspicious haze in the kitchen, and the acrid smell of marijuana. No wonder Larry had thrown open the window. Judy regarded him with unusual coldness.

"You've been smoking marijuana, presumably with one of your friends. You know very well your mother *hates* the idea of your doing any kind of drugs, Larry. She wouldn't even let you smoke in the house, let alone pollute the air with grass."

"I didn't think there was anyone home," he said.

"What kind of an excuse is that? Where did you get the marijuana, Larry?"

The boy shrugged indifferent shoulders. "You can get it anywhere, Judy. It's as easy to buy as cigarettes."

Judy imagined that among city teenagers that was probably true. "Do you still have some here?"

"No. Mik . . . my friend took it with him. Look, Judy, it's no big deal. Everyone does it, like adults drink liquor."

"From the looks of things, you had liquor, too." The door to the cabinet where she and Liza kept their small supply of hard liquor was slightly ajar, and a spill on the table smelled of scotch. "I'd like to know whether this is a habit with you, or an occasional experiment, Larry."

"I've done it before, and I'll probably do it again," he said defiantly. "It's just for fun, Judy. I don't smoke it every day like some of the kids. You have a lot of laughs when you're high. And, God, I get hungry. We ate just about everything in the fridge. But, then, nobody made me dinner."

"Why, you poor dear," she said, raising her brows at him. "Heaven knows that after a hard day of play, you really deserve to come home to a hot meal cooked by someone who worked all day. Makes sense to me."

"I didn't play all day," he insisted, rinsing the last of the dishes. "I worked on Roger's computer, learning a word processing program. And I watered his garden, too."

"Have you almost finished with your hours there?" Judy asked.

"I haven't added them up in the last week, but I

probably only have ten or fifteen left to go. Why? Is he tired of having me around? Did he complain?"

"Of course not. In fact, he's hoping you'll want to spend time doing things together when you've finished." Then Judy remembered the talk she'd had with her sister just before she fell asleep, and her brows drew down. "I think Liza would prefer that you spent time with Phil. They seem to be getting kind of serious."

"Phil," Larry said with youthful scorn. "He's so uptight. Why couldn't Mom find someone cool like Roger? If Mom marries Phil, I won't live with them."

"Where would you live?"

"With you. Couldn't I?"

Judy dropped into one of the kitchen chairs, aware that her headache had returned. "Larry, you know I'd be happy to have you live with me, but that's impractical. Your mother wants you to live with her. Kids almost always have trouble adjusting to stepparents, but it does happen, you know. Phil wants you to like him."

"He doesn't act like it." Larry moved to sit down at the table opposite her. "At dinner the other night, he said everyone with an ounce of intelligence should get a college degree. He thinks my becoming a paramedic is setting my sights too low. Honestly, that's what he said. Like I should become a lawyer or a doctor just because that's more acceptable in his world. He doesn't even know me."

Judy could imagine the scene and could almost feel sorry for the overeager Phil, blundering onto Larry's one real passion. "Phil probably doesn't know much about kids, Larry."

"Well, neither does Roger, but he tries to find out. He probably thinks it would be better for me to be a doctor than a paramedic, but he doesn't go around acting like I'm being stubborn if I don't see it that way. Roger went along with me. Phil couldn't do that."

"Give him time. He probably doesn't understand how important being a paramedic is to you."

"But I *told* him. He just wasn't listening."

Judy cocked her head, surveying him with sympathetic eyes. "Grown-ups almost always think they know better than teenagers, Larry. After all, we've already been through that phase, and we've also been through a lot of years as adults where we've learned some hard lessons about life. Sometimes all an adult is doing is trying to spare you from suffering the same agonies they went through."

"I don't think that's what it is with Phil," he grumbled. "I think being a paramedic isn't classy enough for him."

"You may be right. But even that isn't the end of the world. Larry, you'll be eighteen in a year and a half. That's not so long. And if Phil's likely to be a part of your life, it would be smart of you to try to get along with him."

"Do you really think Mom would marry him?"

"She seems very fond of Phil."

His brows drew down over rebellious eyes. "You don't like him, do you?"

"I've barely met him, Larry. He's attractive and he's intelligent, and he has the good sense to like Liza. That's a pretty good recommendation."

"Humph. Is she out with him now?"

Judy nodded. "But we've gotten away from the marijuana and alcohol, Larry. I'll have to tell Liza about that."

"Oh, great. And she'll tell Phil, who will think he has to straighten me out. Maybe I'll just run away, since no one cares about me around here."

"Your problem is that *everyone* cares about you. And don't even think about running away," Judy pleaded. "You have no idea what happens to kids out on the streets. I've seen them in the emergency room and in the operating room. It's really scary, Larry. If things get to be too much, maybe you could see Dr. Bloom again."

"Now you want to send me to a therapist!" he growled. "You're as bad as the rest of them. I'm going to bed." And he stomped down the hall, slamming the door of his room.

Judy didn't try to cajole him out. She had said as much as she could. It was not so difficult for her to remember being sixteen and having no power to determine her own life. No wonder teenagers were so hard to deal with. They felt fully capable of making their own decisions, but every adult knew they hadn't the foggiest notion of what life was really like. If you were too protective, they didn't learn to fend for themselves. If you were too rigid, they rebelled. If you were too easy on them, they walked all over you.

Judy wiped up the spilled alcohol on the kitchen table, almost regretting that she'd discovered Larry's misbehavior. Because obviously Larry had just set in motion a new series of confrontations with his mother, and probably Phil, and he wasn't going to like the results one bit.

Chapter Sixteen

Between cases Roger called his house to see if Larry was there doing the work he'd suggested the previous day. After a minimal amount of yard work and fussing with the car, Roger had suggested Larry call the local junior and community colleges to find out what courses they offered in EMT basic training. By this time the boy had learned that training required more than one hundred hours of classroom work plus ten hours of internship in a hospital emergency room. He was keeping all the information he gathered in a file on Roger's laptop.

Roger's intent was to help Larry see the progression necessary to achieve his goal. In his search for information, Larry had already discovered that he had to be eighteen and have a high school diploma or equivalent and a driver's license. More to the point, there was a recommendation that prospective

EMTs take health and science courses in high school, and Roger was hoping this would influence the teenager's ordinarily lax attitude toward his final year.

Larry answered the phone at Roger's house, but he was particularly uncommunicative. "I don't know why I'm doing this. No one's going to let me be an EMT anyhow."

"Of course they are. Who would stand in your way?"

"Oh, you don't know anything," the boy mumbled.

Roger was not unused to this type of useless negativity from his protégé. "I'd know if you'd tell me."

"Ask Judy" was all Larry said before he hung up.

Roger determined that he would do precisely that, since he'd been looking for an excuse to talk to her again. He called the oncology floor and found she was working the day shift, which meant she'd be off at four, well before he expected to be finished in the OR. Between the next two cases, he hurried up to Six East and tracked her down.

"We need to talk about Larry," he said abruptly.

"How did you know?"

"He told me to ask you what was going on."

"I see. You could call me tonight."

Roger shook his head. "We should talk in person. Let me take you to dinner."

Judy hesitated, but, apparently seeing his determination, reluctantly agreed. "Pick me up when you're through."

"About seven, then. Maybe a little earlier."

The operation he'd participated in then had been demanding as far as the anesthesia went, with their very nearly losing the patient. Roger didn't have a moment to think about what the problem might be, and he arrived late at Judy's in the partially repaired Audi all unsuspecting.

Though Judy opened the door to him, Roger had never seen her look quite so distracted. She raked short fingers through her curly black hair and said, "Roger, we seem to be in the middle of a family conference. How do I explain all this to you? It's kind of complicated."

"Would you rather we talked tomorrow?"

"Infinitely," she admitted, "but I don't think that would help. Where should I start?"

She waved him to a seat on the carpeted stairs which he took with a look of surprised amusement. She sat down on a riser above and said, "Well, Liza has been seeing this lawyer from her firm, Phil Miller. It sounds like they're getting kind of serious, you know? So she wants him to like Larry, and Larry to like him, and they've gotten off on the wrong foot because . . . well, pretty much what you'd expect. Phil doesn't know anything about teenagers; Larry's bristles are up because he thinks Phil will stop him from becoming a paramedic."

"Why would he?"

"Oh, I don't know," she said, impatient. "Maybe he wouldn't, when push came to shove. But he suggested that Larry should aim higher. Anyhow, that's not the point, Roger."

"Oh. Well, what is the point?"

"Liza thinks that if Phil spends more time with Larry, that they'll get to know each other and like each other."

"It's possible."

"Yes, but she thinks that won't happen if Larry continues to spend time with you." Judy had blurted it out, and now laid a hand on his shoulder. "It's not that she isn't grateful for what you've done, Roger. She is. We both are. It's just that this is important to her."

Roger was startled by how distressed he felt. He had become used to guiding this teenager, to spending time with him, to helping him grow up a little. But it was not just the idea of Larry's being absent from his life that upset him. Without Larry, he would have no real link to Judy. When she removed her hand from his shoulder, he said, "And you think that's a good idea, my bowing out of Larry's life?"

"I don't think it's a good idea at all. Frankly, I think Larry would resent it, and like Phil even less. Though Liza thought maybe you could say you were too busy . . ."

"No, I couldn't do that." Roger tugged at his right earlobe. "He only has a few more hours to finish up."

"Yes, but I know you were hoping to spend time with him afterward." Judy's voice caught, and her eyes looked suspiciously moist. "It *would* be a natural breaking point, though, when he'd finished his 'community service' commitment to you."

"I suppose." Roger felt like a lead weight had descended on his stomach. "I'd have to talk to him, Judy."

"Well, that's not everything," she confessed. "Last night I discovered him in the kitchen, where he'd been smoking marijuana and drinking alcohol with a friend."

"Ouch. What did he say?"

"That everyone did it. That he'd do it if he wanted to, and that he didn't do it all the time."

"The old, defiant Larry. Well, I never supposed that I'd reformed him entirely," he said, a rueful twist to his lips. "So who's dealing with the problem?"

"That's what the family conference is about." Judy motioned with her head to the floor above. "It's going on right now, and Larry insists that you be a part of it."

"No one else must want that."

Judy moistened her lips. "Well, I wouldn't mind, but it's such a mess, Roger. Liza doesn't know quite what to do, so she's putting a lot of pressure on Phil to take a stand. But he's kind of alarmed by the whole scenario and has, I think, visions of a drug-addicted teenager destroying his future. Larry's being sullen and rude. I can't see why you should have to take part in this, but I can't very well walk out of here right now."

Roger rose from his seat on the stairs. "Let's go up," he said, and gave her hand a reassuring squeeze. His stomach growled, but Roger suspected he wasn't going to get dinner anytime soon.

At the living room doorway, he paused as Judy walked into the room. Phil rose and turned toward them. He was a man of above-average height with brown hair graying with distinction at his temples. His suit and tie were impeccable, and probably foreign, his shoes shone even in the evening light. He wore a rather grave expression, but Roger thought Judy was probably right that beneath his solemnity was a fear for his future comfort. He stepped forward and offered his hand to Roger.

"Phil Miller," he said.

"Roger Janek."

Before either of them could say anything further, Larry jumped up from the sofa where he had been sitting with his mother. "Roger, will you talk sense to these people? Phil's talking about putting me in a treatment program, for God's sake. I won't go. I don't need to go. Hell, you'd think I'd been smoking crack. For my generation, smoking marijuana is just like drinking beer was for yours."

"Really?" Roger regarded him with a cool expression. "I don't think so, Larry. Marijuana isn't legal for minors *or* adults, and there's the potential of its becoming addictive and leading to worse drug abuse. Haven't you seen drug abusers in the emergency room, and patients with drug overdoses?"

Larry was obviously angry and resentful, but his ears colored now with something like embarrassment. "Of course I have, but this is different."

"You may want it to be different, but it's a serious matter."

"Hell, Roger, *everybody* experiments with marijuana. You probably have yourself."

"I think we've talked before about the problems of peer pressure. You assured me you didn't feel it." Roger turned away from the boy to greet Liza. "Judy's been explaining the situation to me," he said, giving a certain emphasis to his words that made Liza flush faintly. "I hope you won't mind my joining the discussion. I'd like to do what I can to help. I have to admit, I'm disappointed in Larry."

The teenager scowled at him, saying, "It wasn't peer pressure. I like marijuana. It helps you relax."

"So does exercise, and it's a lot safer for you," Roger rejoined.

Phil had pulled a chair forward for Roger, who now sat down and waved Larry back onto the sofa. Judy had taken a stool off to the side and seemed content to listen for the time being, her deep blue eyes noncommittal. When Phil had reseated himself, he cleared his throat and volunteered his view of the situation.

"You see, it's obvious that Larry has smoked marijuana before. That worries me. Every kid thinks he's the one who's not going to become addicted, that he won't go on to use heavier drugs. That he won't ruin his life." Phil leaned earnestly toward Liza. "But I see it every day, don't I? In a law office like ours we see families, often really wealthy and prominent families, come to us for legal help with their kids who have gotten into trouble with drugs."

Liza nodded. "It scares me, too. I've talked to Larry about drugs and alcohol. He knows how I feel."

"Yes, but from what you've told me, and what I've seen for myself, Larry isn't always under your control." Phil regarded Larry with a worried frown. "If it were my decision to make, which it's not, I realize, I'd insist on a treatment program. That's what most of our clients do for their kids."

Judy looked at Roger, who remained silent, and then said, "But, Phil, that's a different situation. The reason those families are there is because the kids are in legal difficulties around their drug use. That's not the case with Larry. I don't approve of his using marijuana, but I think what you're suggesting is overkill."

"What you have to do is nip these problems in the

bud," Phil insisted. "Look, I'm sure Larry's a good kid. But lots of good kids get mixed-up with drugs. He's already had a brush with the law, remember."

Larry glared at the attorney. "That had nothing to do with marijuana."

Sadly, Phil said, "How do we know that?"

Liza hastened to defend her son. "I'm sure it didn't, Phil. Larry had been with us since he got home from school that day. We'd have smelled it if he'd had marijuana."

Judy added, "And I don't think a drug treatment program would take Larry if he doesn't have a problem. They're for people who are already in trouble with drug use, not for kids who might or might not be using them."

"I'm sure they'd take him," Phil said. "I could probably arrange it through contacts at the office. And I think it's really important that you do it, Liza."

Liza looked torn. Roger could see that she wanted to please Phil, but she also hesitated to take such a drastic action with her son. Her eyes begged Judy to come to her assistance, and Judy finally said, "How about this? Why don't we send Larry to see Dr. Bloom to discuss his use of marijuana and other stresses in his life? That kind of one-on-one attention might me more useful to him."

"I won't go," Larry protested. "He didn't really listen to me when I went before, and he asked stupid questions, like whether I'd hated my father. How dumb can someone be? Then he acted like there was something wrong with me for loving Dad and missing him. He made me feel like a nutcase."

"Oh, I didn't realize that," Liza said. "You didn't tell me, Larry. We could have found someone else."

"I don't want someone else. I want to be left alone." Larry jumped up and ran from the room. They heard his loud footsteps on the stairs, and the slam of the front door.

Phil looked stunned by the turn of events. "Aren't you going to bring him back?" he asked of the room in general.

"How could we do that?" Judy replied, frustrated. "He'll come back when he's cooled off."

Phil moved to take Larry's place on the sofa beside Liza. He grasped her hand and said earnestly, "You've got to exercise some control over him, Liza. You have to make him do what you know is best for him."

"But I don't know what's best, in this situation," she admitted. "I know you think a treatment program is the only thing that would help, but I'm afraid it would just drive him farther away from us, from you, Phil. He'd resent you for doing that to him. And I'm not sure he needs a drug treatment program."

Her gaze moved to Roger, as though in search of his opinion. Phil flinched at this obvious sign of his own lack of weight in the discussion. "I need some time to think all of this through, Liza, and I don't much feel like going out right now. You have to understand that I'm not used to this kind of family crisis. It's hard for me to be in a situation where I don't have any influence in the decisions being made."

"But you do have influence, Phil. It's just that . . . well, you don't know Larry very well yet and the rest of us do and . . ."

He sighed and patted her hand. "Exactly. Look, I'll call you later, okay? Or tomorrow. And we'll talk."

Liza blinked back a sudden rush of tears. "Okay. But really, Phil, I do value your suggestions. It's just . . ."

Phil had already risen, and now, nodding to Judy and Roger, said, "I know. I'll call."

As his footsteps retreated down the stairs, Judy moved to the sofa and handed her sister a tissue to mop up the tears that were now flowing freely. "It will all get sorted out, Liza. You can't blame Phil for feeling frustrated with us. The whole situation is too new for him to grasp all the ramifications."

"I know. I don't blame him. I just . . ." Liza hiccuped and pressed the tissue more firmly against her eyes. "I hate being torn between them, Judy. And I'm afraid it might always be like that. If he's ever willing to give it a try."

"Poor dear." Judy looked up at Roger, who rose immediately.

"I'll run along, too," he said. "We can talk another time, Judy."

"Oh, no!" Liza cried. "You guys go on out to dinner, and forget all about this. I'll be fine."

Though they both declared their readiness to put off their plans, Liza insisted that they go out and leave her. "I need some time to think, too," she said. "It's been an upsetting evening."

Eventually Roger followed Judy down the stairs and out of the building. "Poor Liza. This has to be hard on her," he said as he held the door to the passenger side for Judy.

"Do you think I should have stayed with her?"

He shook his head. "I imagine she really does need some time to think about Phil, and Larry, and the current and future problems." He lowered his window to let in the lush evening air. For a moment he sat staring out the windshield, then shook his head to clear his mind. "Even the simplest things can get really complicated, can't they?" he asked as he started the car.

"Yes. But if you learn to focus on the most important strands, you can usually unravel the mess."

Roger smiled at her. "You're such a sensible woman, Judy. Do you care where we eat?"

"Not much. I'm not a big fish fan."

"Thai okay?"

"Sure."

Roger parked near one of the dozens of restaurants on Geary Boulevard, a Thai place he'd eaten at before. They were seated in the sparsely populated room at a comfortable table by the windows. While Roger went to the bathroom, Judy watched the pedestrians passing on the sidewalk, her mind taken up with her sister's concerns. But when Roger returned and sat down opposite her, she was suddenly very much aware of him.

Judy was vividly reminded that she'd gone home with him after Angel and Cliff's party. What folly to have given in to that momentary desire! But she found now, looking at him, that her body was responding in a similar way. Just sitting here across from him, following the energetic dartings of his hands, the sensuous movement of his lips, the eager fire in his eyes, she could feel a tightening in her throat and in her groin. She remembered his touch in a graphic way that she could not dismiss.

"I've had the curried chicken," he was saying. "I think you'd like it."

Judy lifted one careless shoulder. "That sounds fine." But she could not have told him whether he'd suggested chicken or prawns, satay or rice. *Concentrate,* she admonished herself. *This is not smart. He's here to talk about my nephew and whether he can remain involved in Larry's life. He probably has suggestions for how to handle the current crisis with Larry.*

When Roger had given their order to the waitress, he looked at her curiously. "Are you plotting something?" he demanded. "You look positively mysterious."

Judy felt herself flush. "I was wondering what you thought we should do about Larry."

"And the marijuana? I don't like it, but I tend to agree with you that Phil's idea of a treatment program at this point is excessive. Let me talk to some of the people at the hospital who deal with drug addiction, and see what they recommend. And I'll ask Jerry what he thinks. He could probably recommend a more sympathetic therapist for Larry."

"That would help. And I've been thinking that maybe I could teach Larry ways of dealing with people he finds difficult. Unless you think that would corrupt him."

"Corrupt him? How?"

Judy shrugged. "Well, teaching him how to deal with adults in a way that will work to his advantage smacks of collaborating with the enemy, somehow."

The waitress brought him a beer and Judy a Thai iced tea. She took a sip of her drink and raised her brows. "This is great. I've never had one before."

"How would you do it?" Roger rubbed a hand restlessly over the frosted glass, his brow wrinkled. "What have you learned about dealing with difficult people?"

"I'm a nurse, and I deal with doctors all day."

His hand stilled. "And doctors are difficult people?"

"Sometimes. They may not be difficult with other doctors, but they can be difficult with nurses. They have the authority and the knowledge. But even more important, they have an emotional distance from their patients that a nurse can't afford to have. So sometimes you have to satisfy them on their power level, just so you can maintain your self-respect on a caring level. I think I could teach Larry something useful about dealing with adults while still preserving his sense that he's okay."

"Hold on a minute, Judy. This is important, what you're telling me about how you interact with doctors. Maybe it has something to do with how you feel about me."

"Not really." She kept her voice neutral, meeting his gaze with studied calm. "For a nurse it's survival training, Roger. The trick is to do your job, to please someone who has authority over you, and to find satisfaction on your own level. That takes a certain skill in focusing on what's important and using the means at hand to achieve your own goals."

"Don't you like doctors?"

"I like most of them, most of the time. But doctors have a tendency to think they're the only competent, intelligent people in the hospital. Nurses have to find ways to flourish in that kind of atmosphere, and it's not easy. They have to think of themselves as doing a different job than physicians, not an inferior job."

"Do you think I treat nurses as if they were inferior?"

"Roger, we're not talking about you. We're talking about strategies for surviving in potentially hostile environments, like Larry feels he's in. I'm just saying I think I could help him, given my experience."

Roger twisted the band on his wristwatch, saying, "I can't help but think this has something to do with you and me."

"Well, you're wrong." Judy thanked the waitress as she set down the curried chicken dish and a clay pot with translucent noodles, vegetables, and prawns. As she helped herself to the first dish, she went on, "I don't remember ever seeing you interact with a nurse in a way I didn't approve of, Roger. Besides, the OR is different from the floors. You get to thinking of surgeons as special because of the power they have in the OR, and you respect their authority, if they're decent people, because it's a job you know you couldn't do. I had to make a lot of adjustments when I switched to Six East."

"How?"

"Well, on the floors you know you probably could do their job, except that you wouldn't want to. I don't mean they don't have tons more knowledge, just that given time and effort you could acquire that knowledge, too. I've known several nurses who became doctors. And I respect a doctor's job, it's just that I prefer a nurse's. Doctors don't get to spend much time with patients, they don't get to help with their emotional adjustment to illness, they don't get to be there when they're in pain and need comforting. See, that's more important to me than diagnosing an illness, or ordering a treatment."

"But there's all that other stuff you have to do, like making beds and dealing with bedpans."

"The drudgery, sure, but it's the kind of thing any helpless patient needs, from senile elders to newborn infants."

Suddenly he asked, "Did you know Angel had her baby?"

"Oh, great! Did everything go okay?"

"Fine. It's a boy, and they named him after me."

Judy stared at him. "Well, why didn't you tell me right away? That's great, Roger. So when are you going to meet the little guy?"

"Heaven knows. I got a picture in the mail yesterday." He reached into the inside pocket of the jacket hanging on his chair and drew out a plastic-covered photo of a very young infant. "Roger Crawford Lenzini. He was born on the anniversary of my wedding day."

Her gaze swept up instantly from the child's picture. "What a lovely gesture. He's adorable, isn't he?"

"Well, I don't know how you can tell when they're that young, but since he's Angel and Cliff's kid, I'm sure he'll be a real winner." He accepted the photo back and stuffed it in his pocket once more. "But you were telling me about nurses and doctors, and I've been wondering if your thinking was influenced by what's-his-name."

"You know his name, Roger."

"Okay, Wayne. I don't actually remember his last name, something that began with a *B*, I think."

"Belliver. When we didn't live together anymore, Wayne dealt with me as a nurse, certainly, but he's very good at dealing with people because he respects everyone."

"Do you think I respect everyone?"

"Roger, you're not in some kind of competition with Wayne."

"But how *do* you think of me?"

Judy felt a twinge run through her body. It was hard to regard his earnest brown eyes with anything less than sympathy, but it was more than that. "I'm fond of you, Roger," she said carefully.

"How fond?"

"Eat your dinner."

"But I want to know."

"Just because you want to know something doesn't mean I have to tell you."

"If we were just friends, you'd be able to tell me, wouldn't you?"

Chapter Seventeen

Roger was ignoring his food, and regarding Judy intently. She could feel the heat rise to her face, but she said nothing. What could she say? You turn me on? He didn't need to know that. She couldn't possibly put herself at such a disadvantage, with a revelation that would embarrass him. Besides, he didn't have any right to ask her how she felt about him, since he wasn't in a position to reciprocate any attachment except friendship. She didn't have to satisfy his curiosity.

Very much to her surprise, he said, "Then let me tell you how I feel about you. Every time I see you, I feel this disturbance all through me. Not just, you know, sexual, but everything. My head gets fuzzy, and my hands are like ice." He laid his left hand on her right arm, and it was indeed very cool. "I don't want to get involved with anyone. I'm still mourning for Kerri. But this reaction happens anyhow. I don't seem to have any control over it."

She covered his cold hand with one of her warm ones, but said nothing.

"And then I expected you to be supportive to me, and you let me down. Right when I needed you."

Judy wanted to explain, but explaining would be too revealing. She remained mute.

"Other people have been supportive of me. They've been there when I was a wreck. And you, the one person I really needed to be there—you walked away from me. That really distressed me."

She continued to hold his hand, which had grown warmer now. She was very aware of his skin against hers. Though she counseled caution to her body, it was not remaining neutral. Her gaze never left his face.

Roger unconsciously began to stroke her arm with his thumb. "It wasn't that I couldn't manage the back problem," he said. "It was that you and I had, you know, gotten together and then you just up and left. Abandoned me. Not like Kerri, of course. She had no choice. But you had a choice, Judy. And you just walked away."

"Oh, come on, Roger. There's no similarity between those two things. You were just feeling sorry for yourself."

"No one but Cliff ever tells me I'm feeling sorry for myself. Everyone else is more tactful."

"I don't have to be tactful, Roger. I have to be honest."

He pursed his lips. "What makes you think that's honest? You won't even be honest about how you feel about me."

"You're trying to manipulate me," Judy protested. "There's a difference between my not wanting to tell you how I feel about you, and my being honest with myself about how I feel about you."

"And you think you're being honest with yourself?"

Judy gave a tsk of annoyance. "What I meant was that I had to be true to myself. When I decided I wasn't going to step into Angel's shoes as your comforter, it was because I needed to protect myself. I don't sleep with every man I'm attracted to, Roger. It's a big deal to me. I can't be both lover and sister to you."

"But we'd decided we wouldn't be lovers."

"I don't know that that would have been my choice had your back not gone out. And then I realized that you wanted to forget what had happened. I've never in my life slept with someone I didn't intend to have a relationship with. Maybe this would have been the first time. But I know myself better than to think it was pure chance that I decided to make love with you."

"I thought we agreed ahead of time that it was just a temporary aberration."

"Oh, sure. People do that, Roger, people who

aren't sure how they're going to feel afterward. People who aren't sure their lovemaking will mesh or satisfy them or something like that. You certainly found out in a big way that it wasn't something you should have done. That doesn't mean I did."

"You thought you still wanted to have a relationship with me?"

"Yes, for myself. But the relationship I wanted to have was not as your caregiver. And that's what you expected. That's why you were disappointed in me."

Their fingers had somehow become intertwined. Judy might not have admitted to him that she had wanted the sexual relationship to continue if her body, right now, hadn't begun to ache with an almost painful need to be naked in his arms. She couldn't tell by his awed expression whether he shared her need, or simply was astonished at her being so frank about how she had felt.

He blinked uncertainly. "Do you still feel that way?"

Her body would not allow her to lie. Sensual impulses continued to roam through her. She nodded.

"Do you feel that way right now?"

"Yes."

A slow grin transformed Roger's face. "Me, too. I was afraid it was just me."

Judy looked at the almost full dishes on their table. "Are we going to do anything about it?"

He lifted her hands to his lips and kissed the

palm. "I hope so. But there's no reason not to eat first."

Judy wasn't sure what they talked about after that. Nothing to do with the two of them, certainly. Just general chatter, about Fielding and people they knew and the approaching football season. But she was glad when they were finished, because her body felt too on edge to remain in this public place. Already people seemed to be regarding them curiously, as if they were wearing outlandish outfits or sending off sparks.

Roger, obviously restraining his usual manic style of driving, brought the car safely into his garage and turned off the engine. He came around to hold the passenger door for Judy, and they stood for a moment looking into each other's eyes. He pulled her tightly against him and kissed her, gently at first and then with increasing passion.

Judy felt the heat rise in her again, but she was a little afraid, too, of what would happen now. Not for herself, precisely, except that whatever happened to Roger would affect her, too. They were, once again, in his house. It would have been better if they had gone somewhere neutral—to a motel, even. Upstairs they would encounter all the memories, all the ghosts of his love for Kerri.

Clasping her hand in his, Roger led her up the basement stairs and into the hallway of the main floor. He hesitated there, asking, "Do you want me to get you anything to drink?"

Judy shook her head. Unable to prevent herself, her gaze had wandered into the living room. It looked different, somehow, and she was aware almost immediately that there was no photograph of Kerri there now. Roger had already begun to climb the stairs to the second floor, and she followed him, puzzled.

In the bedroom, Roger walked over to close the blinds on the street side of the house. It was still light enough out that they didn't need to turn on the room lights.

Roger kissed her forehead, and the tip of her nose. His lips found hers in a sweet kiss that made her breathing quicken. Every part of her body was aware of the place it was pressed against his, as if his need and hers were interlocked. Her breasts felt particularly sensitive tight against his chest, and the hard bulge of his penis awakened turmoil in her groin. For a long time they stood that way, their lips exploring, their bodies becoming lush with desire.

Finally he took her hand and tugged her toward the bed. But not in a hurried, out-of-control manner. "Sit on the bed with me," he suggested. "Let me look at you. Let me get to know the feel of your skin, and your touch on mine. You're not too shy to do that, are you?"

Judy shook her head and laughed. "Not when I'm

feeling like this." She seated herself opposite him, cross-legged as he was, and for a while they simply drank each other in. When he began to take off his shirt, she started to remove her blouse. It felt perfectly natural for him to reach across and unhook her bra. Her breasts, freed from their confinement, seemed to burgeon with the need to be touched. But for a while he simply looked at her, and smiled.

His chest was covered with coarse brown hair that tickled her fingers as she stroked it. He had a surprisingly broad chest for such a lanky man, and a waist that looked narrow in comparison. Judy unbuttoned the top of his trousers and slid the zipper down only part way. His patch of rough brown hair there peeked out, sending a surprising thrill through her.

Roger unzipped her skirt and pushed it down, just about the same distance. He looked up to catch her gaze, his face wonderfully alight with pleasure. No shadow darkened its openness. "This is like strip poker," he said, grinning.

"Did you ever play that when you were a kid?"

He nodded. "Yeah, I remember there was a girl next door who challenged me to a game when I was thirteen. She must have been a few years older. It was the first time I'd seen a girl naked right in front of me."

"What happened?"

"Not too much. She was naked first. I don't think

she tried very hard to keep any clothes on." Roger shook his head reminiscently. "Not that she left me any of my own. When her clothes were all off and she still lost, her rule was that I could touch her breast."

"Did you like that?"

"Yeah. I could hardly believe what was happening. I thought it meant we were going to have sex."

"But it didn't."

"No. In fact, I think the whole point of the exercise was for her to touch my penis. She wanted to see my erection. That seemed to fascinate her."

"It would fascinate me, too," Judy said. "About now."

"Would it?" He pretended to consider the possibilities and finally said, "Will you take off the rest of your clothes if I do?"

"Sure."

Roger retrieved a condom from the drawer. Then they watched each other discard their remaining items of clothing and returned to their seated positions. Judy watched Roger slip on the condom. Her body had become taut with expectation. She reached across for his hand and brought it to her breast, sighing as his fingers cupped the tender flesh. She unfolded her legs and moved to wrap them around his waist, bringing the two of them closer.

Slowly, he rained kisses down her neck and chest, working gradually toward her breasts. When she thought she couldn't bear the suspense any longer, he took a nipple into his mouth and drew on it. Desire coalesced in her groin. She reached out to touch Roger, to clasp his penis and stroke it. He moaned with pleasure.

Naked, locked to each other by the needs of their bodies, they swayed together in a parody of dancing, the rhythm slowly intensifying. Judy could feel his penis between her legs, rubbing against her clitoris. His breathing had become as ragged as hers. Almost before she realized it, since it was the most natural thing in the world, they were joined more intimately, shifting into a face-to-face position on the bed, allowing the inevitable to work its magic.

His lips clung to hers, his arms held her close as the tension rose higher, and higher. And then, in a burst of ecstasy, Judy experienced a profound release. She held tightly to Roger, swaying to his rhythm, and realized that he, too, had come. Together they snuggled close, murmuring soft words of happiness and satisfaction.

After a long time Judy said, "How's your back?"

And Roger laughed, and sighed, and drew a heart on her cheek with a steady finger. "It's fine. Were you worried?"

"Weren't you?"

"At first. But then I forgot all about it."

"I'm glad." Judy drew herself up on one elbow and

studied his face. "Would you be more comfortable if I went home now?"

"Good Lord, no. I want you to spend the night, if that's okay with you. Stay here and we can find fun things to do in the morning."

"Like discover where all our clothes have gotten to?"

"That reminds me," he said, frowning. He rolled over, turned on the bedside lamp, and dug in the drawer of the nightstand. After a moment he came out with a piece of gold jewelry in the palm of his hand. "This is yours, isn't it? When my back was better and I was searching for a pair of shoes under the bed, I found that. I meant to return it to you but . . ." He shrugged, looking embarrassed. "I didn't want to get rid of it, somehow."

Judy rubbed the gold earring between her fingers. "Yes, it's mine. I'd put it in the pocket of my pants. The other one must still be there. I haven't worn them since."

"You took them off at the party. You wouldn't tell me why."

"Wayne had given them to me. Seeing him there, and knowing that he didn't even remember, that he wouldn't care . . . I don't know. I just didn't feel like wearing them any more."

"I see." Roger drew his finger across her lips. "We both have a lot of baggage, don't we?"

"Hey, we're in our thirties. Who wouldn't?"

"But it's pretty heavy baggage," he persisted. "You changed where you worked and the kind of nursing you did because of Wayne. That's no small thing."

"It wasn't just because of him." Judy gave him a reluctant smile. "Well, a lot of it was. But it's certainly turned out well for me. I like floor nursing better than working in the OR. But, you know, Roger, Wayne has come to my rescue twice since he's been at Fielding, and it makes me feel a little strange."

"How, strange?"

"Oh, I don't know. As if he'd become my protector or something. He doesn't owe me anything."

"But you have a past together."

"Well, he wasn't coming to my rescue when we first broke up."

Roger drew his finger down the length of her nose. "That would have been hard, wouldn't it?"

"I don't know, but I certainly don't expect him to now," she said with a stubborn tilt to her chin.

"Men are such jerks," he said, kissing the stubborn chin.

"You bet they are," she agreed as she cuddled closer to him. "It's hard to see how women put up with them."

"I know," Roger said as his lips trailed down toward her breast.

Roger dropped Judy off at her flat on his way to work, very early the next morning. Instead of the divine retribution that he had half expected, his back was strong and his heart was beating quite merrily. In fact, he hadn't felt this happy in ages. It was almost as if he'd been seeing the world through gauze the last year, and at last he was seeing with clear, unhampered eyes. Everything looked sparkling fresh, like a rainwashed landscape through newly cleaned windows.

He hurried into scrubs in the men's dressing room, which at Fielding had been auditorily linked to the women's OR dressing room so the male and female surgeons could discuss their cases while they changed. Roger missed finding himself there with Cliff many mornings; his rapport with the other surgeons was excellent, but not as close personally. Today he discovered that he would be working with Wayne Belliver. Maybe this was his divine retribution after all?

Wayne remembered him from the party, and remembered that he had been there with Judy. Roger had forgotten how homely Wayne was, and how nice. Very few surgeons—face it, no surgeons—Roger knew were that good-hearted and generous. The man offered him a pack, not a piece, of gum when he admitted to digging in his pants pocket in search of some.

"You're Judy's friend," he said, smiling. "I saw her up on the floor the other day. One of the residents is giving her a bit of guff. I think we should beat him up. What do you say?"

Since the fellow was smiling broadly, Roger understood this to be a mere pleasantry. "Anytime you like," he agreed. "But Judy's pretty good at taking care of her own problems."

"True." Wayne tied the drawstrings at his waist and slammed shut his locker door. "I was surprised she left the OR. She was really good both circulating and scrubbing. Did you ever work with her?"

"A couple of years ago." Roger popped a stick of gum in his mouth and offered Wayne the pack back, but the cardiothoracic surgeon waved it aside, so Roger dropped it in his scrub pants. "She likes it on the oncology floor. I think it's because she has more autonomy there."

"Yes, but it must be awfully depressing. You'd think it would drag you down."

"Not Judy," Roger said, feigning knowledgeability. He wanted, suddenly, to know Judy better than this man beside him did. In fact, he didn't like it at all that Wayne knew her as well as he did. Roger was not jealous in the obnoxious male sense of resenting that this man had had sex with Judy. That didn't bother him particularly. But that Wayne knew Judy intimately in other ways, that he knew stories from her childhood, and how her mind worked—that he *did* resent. He wanted to be the one who knew Judy best, and he knew almost nothing about her, other than what he'd seen over the last two months at a distance.

"Well, I'm glad she likes doing what she's doing. That's great." Wayne slipped paper booties over his shoes. "This is going to be a tough case, Roger. You talked with Mr. Shibbon yesterday, I suppose."

"Yes. He looked almost too sick to operate on."

"He is, but he insists. It's his last chance, and I'm willing to give it to him. But we should talk about afterward, if he survives. I notice that at Fielding they're taking the endotracheal tube out the same day to save on respirator and ICU costs. I don't think that would be wise with him, but I'd like your feedback."

The man was obviously as tactful and thoughtful as Judy had suggested. He and Wayne stood talking for some time about the responsibilities of extubation and who would place the intra-arterial and central venous monitoring lines for the surgery. Wayne solicited his preferences on equipment for putting anesthetic gases into the heart-lung machine and what kinds of drugs he used to stimulate the heart coming off cardiopulmonary bypass.

"One more thing," Wayne said. "I've heard you have a great sound system in the operating room. Could I put in a request for a little country and western? Not the whole time, but a tape or two."

"Sure. I have several. I like a little bit of everything. I keep changing it every half hour or so."

"Sounds great. Thanks." Wayne turned to go and then turned back, almost reluctantly. "Judy and I . . . Did she tell you about us?"

"Yes. She said you'd lived together for a while."

"Good. I like things out in the open." He patted the pocket of his scrub shirt as though he were searching for something. Without looking up, he said, "I was really stupid about that, and I'm afraid I hurt her. She deserves to have the best."

"Yes. She does."

Wayne nodded and turned back toward the door. Roger followed him into the OR, wondering if he'd just been admonished to treat Judy properly, or warned that Wayne was still interested in her.

Chapter Eighteen

When Judy arrived back at her flat, she found her sister in the kitchen, drinking a cup of coffee. Judy helped herself to the last serving in the pot and sat down opposite her. To her surprise, Liza was looking bright-eyed and cheerful. "I take it you and Phil have talked," Judy said.

Liza smiled impishly. "And I take it you spent the night at Roger's."

"Yes. You didn't worry about me, did you?"

"Oh, no. About an hour after you left, Phil called and I went over to his place. We had a really long talk, about us and about Larry, and everything."

"I'm glad. He seemed upset when he left."

"He was. After all, he's a lawyer, and they expect to be in charge of things. And he's really smart, Judy, so he's used to people paying attention to what he has to say."

Her sister nodded. "I know he was trying to help, but he doesn't know Larry the way the rest of us do."

"He admitted that when we talked. And he confessed something he'd never mentioned before. When he was married, he and his wife decided they didn't want children. He just didn't think he was cut out to be a father, because his own dad had been one of those workaholics who never spent any time with his kids. Phil puts in a lot of hours, too, but I don't think he's obsessive about it."

"I wouldn't think so. He's found time for you."

"Yes, he has, hasn't he? But you see, Judy, even his going with me is kind of a compromise for him, because of Larry." Liza ducked her head self-consciously. "I mean, if we were to stay together, he'd have to live with Larry and be like a father to him."

Judy grinned. "At least he wouldn't want you to have any more kids."

"Thank God. Larry is more than enough for me to handle."

"Fortunately, Larry's almost grown."

"I think that's why he was willing to consider it, the two of us getting together." Liza flushed. "And he still is, Judy."

"Well, well. That sounds very encouraging. Tell me what's happened."

"He wants me to move into his house." Liza's pixie face contracted with concern. "Just me, though, so we can get to know each other without all the stress about Larry. What Phil would insist on would be Larry coming to family therapy with us during that time, to see if we couldn't work out some of these problems—the marijuana, the role Phil would be taking over, all that stuff. And then, if things worked out okay, we'd get married."

"Oh, Liza! That's wonderful."

"It wouldn't be a fancy wedding, since we've both been married before. Just a justice of the peace and a few friends and family. But it all means asking a big favor of you. We wondered if Larry could live here with you during that time, and maybe while we took a honeymoon. I know it's asking a lot."

"Nonsense. I'd be glad to do it. And I'm delighted for you, Liza."

"Thanks. I'm kind of walking with my head in the clouds, Judy. I didn't know if Phil would want to take on all my problems." Liza laughed. "Remember I told you how I thought he'd want someone more, oh, educated and socially adept? Because he's kind of ambitious, you know. And I talked about that with him, and he said I shouldn't worry about it. He thought maybe I could work part-time and go to college—if I wanted to."

"Do you?"

"Very much. I've always felt a little behind everyone else. And since he's already got a great house out in the Sunset, and he makes a good living, he can't see why I shouldn't do that. Phil thought a teenager would like to be on a different floor than we are, so Larry can have the den behind the dining room for his bedroom."

"That sounds like a good arrangement."

"I feel a little like Cinderella," her sister confessed. "I mean, me marrying a San Francisco lawyer. He teaches me all kinds of things, like how to dress for special occasions I've never learned about and how politics work in an office like ours."

"Do people at work know you're dating?"

"Oh, sure. We haven't made any secret of it. Phil likes to be up front about things. I think that's the best way to handle it, don't you?"

"Definitely."

"It could be difficult if things didn't work out, but I don't think that will happen." Liza glanced at the clock and jumped up. "God, I've got to get to work. Later you'll tell me about Roger, okay?"

"I'm not sure how much there is to tell," Judy said, "except that I really like him."

At the end of the day Roger received a message on his voice mail from Larry, insisting that the boy needed to see him right away. Roger didn't know of any developments since the previous evening, so he called the flat and got Larry, who agreed to meet him at his house in an hour. When he asked for Judy, he was told she wasn't home yet.

How much would a teenager know or guess about

their relationship? Roger wondered. And where was Judy? Her shift would have been over more than an hour ago. Damn, he wished he'd had time to go by Six East to see her during the day, but he'd had a frantic schedule all day.

"Leave her a message that I called, will you?" he said to Larry.

"Okay, but she's going to be on Mom's side, isn't she? She's her sister, after all."

Roger didn't know precisely what this meant, but he was willing to wait until he got home to find out.

He arrived home to an empty house with dishes in the sink and an unmade bed. Unlike the last time, these evidences of Judy's presence did not frighten and upset him. In fact, he wished fervently that she was there. No light blinked on his answering machine, and he wondered again where she'd gotten to. He wanted her to be there with him.

Larry arrived in a fret. He had ridden his skateboard over and left it outside the front door, saying, "I'll bet Phil doesn't approve of skateboards. He'd probably make me wear some helmet like an eighth-grade sissy."

Roger asked if he'd remembered to leave a message for Judy, and the boy grimaced at him. "You told me to, so I did. Why does everyone think I'm not capable of taking care of the smallest thing?"

"Maybe because for a long time you didn't bother

to take care of the smallest thing," Roger suggested, leading the teenager into the living room, where he waved him to a chair. "Tell me what the problem is."

"Mom and Phil are talking about getting married, and I don't want her to marry him."

"I'm constantly astonished at how self-centered young people are," Roger said. "Your mother, who is most directly involved in this, is probably extremely happy with this turn of events."

"Phil is totally rigid and unsympathetic. He doesn't know anything about kids. Everything's a big deal, and he wants to have his say about it. That's probably why he's marrying Mom, so he can boss me around."

"I hardly think so," Roger said dryly.

"Well, he'll make life miserable for me. I don't know how my mom can do it. My dad hasn't been dead even two years!"

"Life moves on, even when you don't quite expect it to, or want it to, Larry. Your father wouldn't have wanted either you or your mother to grieve for him forever."

Larry thrust out a stubborn chin. "How do you know?"

"Because my wife died not so long ago, and I've been working my way through my grief, too."

The teenager flushed slightly. "Well, it's not the same thing. My father was really special, not like other kids' fathers."

"I'm sure he was. Which is even more reason to believe he'd want your mother and you to be happy."

"Well, I'm *not* happy."

"Try to be, for your mother's sake. You know, Larry, if you're going to make it as an adult, you have to at least pretend to care about other people. It's called getting along in the world. You're going to find out one of these days that the rest of the world doesn't care nearly as much about you as you do, with the possible exception of your mother and your aunt."

"Not you, either?" Larry asked, looking hurt.

"Present company always excepted. But, no, I'm not as interested in your welfare as you are—that would be impossible." Roger grinned at the youngster, taking only a smidgen of the sting out of his words. "People have their own problems, and usually they're a lot more basic than you'd expect. They worry about keeping their jobs and whether they'll have enough money for the rent and the groceries and a new shirt. They don't have time to worry about whether a snot-nosed teenager has a car to drive to school."

This had been one of Larry's more outrageous complaints when he first explained to Roger why he made such a nuisance of himself in the spring. "Everyone else has a car," he had said, perfectly inaccurately. Roger had laughed at him and let the boy know he wasn't concerned with hearing reasons for bad behavior; he was interested in seeing the behavior improve.

Larry regarded him earnestly. "Look, Roger, I've figured the whole thing out. There's one perfect solution to this problem, and it's staring us in the face."

"Really? What is it?"

"I'll come to live with you!"

"Now, see, that's exactly what I meant." Roger shook his head wonderingly. "You think that would be the perfect solution. The fact that your mother would hate it, Phil would reject it, Judy would disapprove, and I have no intention of taking on a full-time teenager, has never crossed your mind."

"You wouldn't want me to live here?" Larry asked, astonished.

"It would be totally inappropriate."

"But you have this whole big house, and you're lonely since your wife died. I'd help out around the place, you know. I'd do the dishes and help with the yard work. Mom would save money 'cause she wouldn't have to feed me. And she wouldn't be worried because she thinks you're a great influence."

"Your mother loves you, and she expects you to live with her. For God's sake, Larry, you're only sixteen."

"I'll be seventeen in five months. And I'm a senior in high school this fall. That's practically grown-up."

Roger sighed. "Larry, I enjoy spending time with you. I'm interested in helping you with your problem about Phil, but there's no way you're going to come here to live."

Larry's face had taken on a dark flush, part anger, part embarrassment. "Well, I guess we know where you stand, don't we?" He jumped to his feet, almost knocking over the chair on which he'd been sitting. "You were the one who wanted to get involved in my life. I've heard my mom and Judy talking. Even before I took your car, you were going to 'help' me. Big help you are! If my mom marries Phil, I'm going to run away! See if I don't."

Larry bolted for the door, paying no attention to Roger's soothing remark. As he banged out of the house, he yelled, "You're just as bad as everyone else! What a dope I was to trust you."

Roger could hear the clatter of his skateboard as Larry spun down the street toward the corner. By the time Roger reached the door and pulled it open, Larry was already turning the corner into the traffic on Sacramento Street, recklessly vying for space with the oncoming cars. Though Roger knew he could catch up with the boy in his car, he knew just as well that Larry, in his present mood, might behave even more recklessly if confronted.

Why was it that he'd wanted to work with a teenage boy in trouble? Roger was hard-pressed, at the moment, to remember. The least he could do, he decided, was to call Liza and tell her about the flare-up, and have her let him know when Larry arrived home safely. If he did.

As he reached for the phone, it rang. Judy sounded a little hesitant. "There's a message here from Larry saying that he was going to your house and that I should call. Is something the matter?"

Roger explained, as simply as possible, what had happened. Judy sounded dismayed that Larry would suggest such a thing as his living with Roger. "I don't know if that indicates how much he dislikes Phil, or how much he likes you, or how much he doesn't care if he hurts his mother's feelings." There was a brief pause, and then she said, "I'll give you a call when he gets here, Roger, so you'll know he's okay."

"I was hoping to see you tonight."

"Maybe later. I . . ."

There was a loud hammering at Roger's door, and shouts of his name. Even on the other end of the line, Judy could hear it well enough to say, "That sounds like Larry."

Roger carried the portable phone with him when he hurried to open the door. Larry was indeed there, but obviously the worse for wear. "I'll have to call you back, Judy. He's had an accident."

Though Roger had assured her there was nothing desperate about the situation, Judy immediately drove to his house, experiencing a variety of emotions. Her feelings for Roger seemed altogether too straightforward, given his situation. Judy was well aware that Roger had not expected to find another woman in his life—probably not ever, and certainly not a year after his beloved wife died. And then there was Larry cluttering up the landscape with his demands and his consideration of only himself. Not that that was so unusual for a kid his age, but it certainly muddied the waters where her relationship with Roger was concerned.

By the time she pulled into Roger's driveway, Judy felt nothing so much as exhausted by her unruly emotions. She found the front door left slightly ajar and followed the sound of voices to the kitchen. Without making her presence known, she paused in the doorway to observe the scene.

Roger was in the process of cleaning a bloody scrape on Larry's chin, at the same time answering Larry's eager questions about a mental status examination. "So what does it mean if they can't tell you where they are or who they are?" he asked. "Does it mean they've got a concussion?"

"Maybe. Not necessarily." Roger seemed to sense her presence, and he turned around and smiled a smile so warm and intimate that Judy's heart bounced. "Ah, Judy is here. Now we'll get some real nursing."

Larry looked embarrassed. "I'm okay, Judy. You didn't go telling Mom that I fell, did you? I don't want her to worry."

"Liza was going out to dinner tonight. I haven't seen her." Judy moved closer to her nephew, surveying the damage. "What happened?"

"I hit the edge of the sidewalk trying to get out of the way of some crazy driver," Larry said. "And they think kids can't drive!"

"You aren't supposed to ride your skateboard in traffic," Judy reminded him.

"Where the hell am I supposed to ride it?" he demanded, but a quick look at Roger made him change his attitude. "I know. I'm sorry. When I left here I was mad, and I didn't pay enough attention to what I was doing."

Judy's brows rose at this admission of guilt. "Wow. I don't think I've ever heard you say 'I'm sorry' before. It kind of warms the cockles of my heart."

Larry snorted with laughter, and Roger applied a coat of iodine to the chin, saying, "He's also remorseful for being rude and storming out of here, aren't you, Larry?"

Grinning, the boy said, "Yeah. I was just disappointed. You won't tell Mom I didn't want to live with her, will you, Judy? I didn't mean it like that, really. I just hate the idea of Phil trying to be like a father to me. Roger says he'll help me find ways of coping with him, if that's okay with you."

"So long as you don't undermine Liza's relationship with Phil."

"Nothing like that," Roger assured her, looking up

from his inspection of Larry's torn shirt. His eyes seemed especially bright, his gaze intent and almost questioning. "They have every right to be interested in each other. Who understands where attraction comes from? Not me, for sure."

"Me, either." Judy moved closer to him, ostensibly to pick up a gauze pad he'd dropped on the floor. "So how is Larry going to deal with Phil?"

"Well, the first thing he needs to work on is his tone of voice."

Larry cocked his shaggy head inquisitively. "Why is my tone of voice so important?"

"Because adults like to believe that they respect each other—often they do—and they especially believe that younger people should respect them. If you can manage to keep your voice respectful, no matter what you say, you'll have a better chance of being heard."

"Do you think Larry could learn to do that with Liza and me, too?" Judy asked, half smiling.

"It wouldn't do him a bit of harm, would it? Even when you and I, as grown-ups, don't feel particularly respectful of the people we deal with, we know we have to act as if we do. That's just one of the lessons everyone has to learn to get along in life."

"It doesn't sound so hard," Larry said. "I bet I could do that."

Judy considered him with narrowed eyes. "But there are lots of people we do respect, Larry. I'd hate to teach you a way to get around learning that there are plenty of people out there of real value."

"Hey, I respect some people," the boy protested, running a hand through his spiky hair. "But I expect people to respect me, too."

Roger set the bottle of iodine on the counter and said, "They'll be a lot more likely to do it if you give them some reason to."

Judy nodded. "That means not only doing a good job, which is part of the battle, but dealing with all different kinds of people. If you're going to be a paramedic, you'll have to learn how to accept orders from doctors, even if you don't agree with them. Respectfully suggesting alternatives gets you a lot farther than acting hostile."

Roger leaned back against the kitchen counter, so close to Judy that their hips were touching. "Like Phil thinking you should be a doctor or a lawyer instead of a paramedic. Your job is to change his mind. You can make yourself miserable by flaunting your differences in Phil's face, or you can sit down with him and respectfully go over your strengths and your interests."

"Help him understand that you don't want to be a doctor or a lawyer or something that requires super-academic qualifications," Judy suggested.

"You mean, like make him think I'm too dumb?"

"No, I don't mean that at all. Show him you're more action-oriented and less academically inclined."

Judy turned to Roger for help. "Don't you think that's perfectly legitimate?"

He grinned at her. "Are you trying to tell me something, Judy? Of course I think it's perfectly legitimate."

Larry frowned. "He'll think I'm not going to make enough money being an EMT."

"Well, as long as you're not going to be asking him or your mother to support you for the rest of your life, that's not really a problem." Roger slid his hand into Judy's behind her back where Larry couldn't see.

"A bigger problem," Judy said, switching her gaze from Roger to Larry, "is that paramedics burn out. It's a young person's job. Think of the paramedics you've seen. In case Phil happens to bring that up, you need to think about what you'll do when you're older."

Larry looked confused. "Well, what *would* I do? I hadn't thought about that. There isn't anything that interests me."

"Check in that occupation outlook stuff we found." Roger squeezed Judy's hand and received an answering pressure. "There are all kinds of medical-technician possibilities, nursing, as well as the whole range of nonmedical things: computers, business. You don't have to have all the answers for Phil, Larry. You just have to let him know you've thought of these issues ahead of time."

"And with people who are particularly hard to deal

with, sometimes you have to guide them to reaching the same conclusion you have."

"Like manipulating them," Larry said.

"No, like being subtle and persuasive."

"Is that what nurses do?"

Judy shrugged. "When you're lower down on the ladder, you have to be more circumspect about letting someone know what you want. That just makes good sense. If you want to be the one who wields power, you have to go a different route. You're lucky. You've stumbled on a profession where you'll have a maximum amount of autonomy in a limited but demanding setting."

"Yeah." Larry grinned. "Thanks, you guys. This might actually help me." He eyed the two of them suspiciously. "Is there something going on between the two of you?"

"Well . . ." said Judy.

"Yes," said Roger.

"I thought so. You look like you want to be alone."

"Very perceptive of the boy," Roger conceded. "So leave us alone, Larry. You can take the Audi."

Chapter Nineteen

When Larry had left them alone, Roger gave an exaggerated sigh of relief. He pulled Judy to him and kept her encircled by his arms. "We need to talk." But instead he kissed her. It was a gentle kiss, exploratory and questioning.

She returned his kiss with enthusiasm, but stepped back after a few minutes and said, "Yes, we should talk."

"Right now?"

After a brief hesitation, she nodded. "Yes, right now while our heads are still clear."

"Are they?"

"More or less."

They had remained in the kitchen after Larry left, but now Roger suggested the living room. "Want a drink?" he asked.

Judy shook her head but opened the refrigerator door. "Well, maybe a soda. May I help myself?"

"I don't want you to have to ask me that. I want you to act like this is your house."

She peered at him over the refrigerator door. "But it isn't, Roger. Just like my flat isn't yours. You'd ask at my place."

"I suppose." He watched as she took a diet Coke from the shelf and looked questioningly at him. "Sure. I'll have one, too." He pulled a bag of miniature pretzels down from the shelf and poured them into a bowl. "This might hold us for a few minutes."

"Do you want me to make something for dinner?" she asked.

"No, I don't want you to make something for dinner," he said, upset. "That wasn't what I meant at all. I don't want you to take care of me!"

"Seems to me you did, not so long ago when we talked."

"Well, I was wrong." Roger felt edgy, and he tugged at his right earlobe. "That was something different, anyhow. I felt like you abandoned me. Oh, hell, that's not what I mean, either."

Judy looked at him questioningly. "I don't know where all this is leading, Roger. Did you want to tell me last night was a mistake, too?"

Roger remembered quite clearly her offering to call the first time they slept together a mistake. Of course, it hadn't been; he just hadn't been able to see it yet. She looked now as if he'd just hurt her, taken away something that she had thought was safe. "No! Last night was wonderful. You're wonderful. But we need to talk."

"So you've said." She preceded him into the living room and sank down at one end of the sofa. "So talk."

Roger sat at the other end of the sofa and pushed the bowl of pretzels toward her on the coffee table. "What you said just now to Larry—it was important. It bothers you that I'm a doctor, doesn't it?"

"No. Well, yes, I suppose it does, in some ways."

"Like what?"

"Doctors have a built-in sense of their own importance. It's fostered in their training and encouraged in their practice. When I lived with Wayne, there was never any question that his work was more important than mine, that his hours were more demanding than mine, that our goals were his goals. For someone like me, that wasn't really a healthy situation. It was all too easy to fall into that kind of trap. It took me a long time to work my way back up to feeling significant after he left me."

"That doesn't have to happen."

"If it happened with Wayne, who is probably one of the most considerate men on earth, why should it be different with you, Roger?"

Roger found that he hated being compared with Wayne. He realized that Judy was merely trying to point out that she'd had trouble maintaining her identity with Wayne, but he didn't want to know about any of Wayne's virtues. If old Wayne was considerate, Roger was sure he himself could be twice as considerate. If he tried. If he thought about it.

"Anesthesiologists are different than surgeons, Judy. We don't have the same egos. In fact," he said ruefully, "we can't afford to have much ego at all, in the OR. We do our job without much glory."

"But for a lot of money. And money talks in our world."

"Hey, the way things are going, the money will decrease rather dramatically over the next few years." Roger reached across to take her hand. "I'm just a guy, Judy. I respect what nurses do, and I respect you—always."

"Even in the morning, huh?" she said, shaking her head. "Oh, Roger, it's not you I'm worried about. It's me. I like taking care of people and in my personal relationships I tend to get caught up in that."

He regarded her curiously. "You didn't do that when my back went out."

She sighed. "I know. But I had to work at it. And that was for my own protection. If I had become your nurse, or your confidante, what would have happened to me if I was falling in love with you?"

"Were you? Are you?"

"No fair. We're having a theoretical discussion here."

"Are we?" He stroked her hand with his thumb. "What I feel about you is not theoretical, Judy."

"No, but it's largely sexual."

He shook his head. "I don't think so, and I've been giving it a lot of thought today."

"We haven't known each other long enough to know how we feel," she said. "There are too many confusing elements—like Kerri and Larry and Wayne and doctors and nurses. I can't see things clearly yet, and I don't think you should even try to."

"But I *feel* clearly. I feel this incredible attraction to you, Judy. And it isn't just sexual." His eyes urged her to hear him, to understand. "There's something about you that's so real and so human and so perfectly complementary to me."

"Because I'm not perfect," she said, teasing, but half in earnest.

"That's why we're good for each other. I'm not perfect, either. Kerri was perfect, and Wayne is perfect, or as near as people get, but you and I aren't. We're just bumbling our way through life, trying to do good and hoping we don't screw up. We want to be happy, we want to laugh and cry and get the most out of every day." He regarded her with a question in his eyes. "Or am I just reading things into you that I want to be there?"

"No, that's how I am. I've never thought of it as a particularly endearing quality about myself, though, bumbling through life."

"You know what I mean. You take life as it comes to you. You don't whine about the bad stuff and you don't downplay the good stuff. You're practical and generous and open."

"*Now* you're exaggerating," she protested. "I'm just a regular person, Roger."

"But a special one to me. Aren't I kind of special to you?"

"Now you're fishing." Judy drew a finger along the outline of his jaw. "Yes, you're very special to me, Roger. But there's so much we don't know about each other, and a lot of what we do know is complicated. We'll just take it easy, okay?"

Roger captured her in his arms. "Okay. For now."

For the next few weeks Judy simply enjoyed the time she spent with Roger. She tried not to think ahead, and she managed not to dwell on the past. They spent more time together than she would have thought possible given their busy and not always synchronized schedules.

The night before Liza was planning on moving over to Phil's house, she and Judy were talking in the kitchen when the doorbell rang. "That's probably Phil. He thought we could take some of my stuff over there tonight, and finish in the morning," Liza said, and hurried down to let him in.

When they returned, Phil greeted her and then asked, "How come Larry isn't doing the dishes?"

"He made dinner," Liza explained. "Meatloaf, sort of."

"Or maybe it was supposed to be sloppy joes," Judy said.

Liza laughed and tucked her hand through Phil's arm. "We're going to see a movie tonight. One of Phil's clients recommended it."

Phil grimaced. "It's one of those arty flicks, but everyone seems to be talking about it. I thought we'd ask Larry if he wants to come, but I doubt if he will."

The doorbell rang again, and Judy put down the sponge she was using. "I'll get it. It's probably Roger."

As she made her way down the hall, she dried her hands on a terry-cloth dish towel. At the foot of the stairs, she found that her pulse had speeded up just in anticipation of seeing him. Through the frosted glass she could make out his wiry build and the waves of his curly hair. She pulled open the door to find him smiling, his hands filled with late-summer flowers from his garden. A shock of realization raced through her: she loved this man. She was no longer at the stage where she could prevent herself from losing her heart. It had already happened.

To prevent him from seeing this patent truth, she buried her face in the flowers, murmuring with pleasure. He kissed her forehead, saying, "The garden looks absolutely perfect today. Like you."

She shook her head in pretend disapproval. "Hardly. And I've got dishpan hands."

"Working your fingers to the bone again. I'll help."

"No need. I'm almost done." She turned to head up the stairs and then paused. "Phil's here. Liza's moving in with him tomorrow."

"Is everything okay with Larry?"

"I think so. He's been trying hard to get along with Phil."

"Good. Tell me. I'm all ears."

Judy reached out to give his ear a playful tug. "Not *all* ears, thank goodness."

"Near enough."

Judy tucked the giant bouquet under her chin and started up the stairs before him. "He's played tennis with Phil, and agreed in principel to do family therapy with them, after the two of them have had a few sessions of their own. I think he's counting on their not actually managing to do that."

"Poor deluded child. I'd say Phil is determined to make this work."

"I agree. But he's still very awkward with Larry and a little heavy-handed in the advice department."

At the head of the stairs she stopped and turned to Roger. He was a few steps behind her, and she had to resist the impulse to run her fingers through his hair. "With Liza moving tomorrow, I'm going to have to spend more time here, with Larry."

"That's not going to keep us from seeing each other, Judy. And you know I'll be happy to spend more time with Larry, too."

She nodded and led him into the kitchen, where he offered his hand to Phil. "Roger," Phil said as he shook his hand. "I was sorry to mess up your plans the other day, but I'd already arranged to play tennis with Larry."

"No problem. He needs to play against a variety of adults who won't go easy on him."

Judy was busy arranging the flowers in a large vase at the sink, and she smiled at Roger, who moved closer to her. "Anything I can help with?" he asked.

"You could put this on the side table in the living room while I finish rinsing off the flatware. The flowers are gorgeous, Roger. Are they from your own garden?"

"Yeah. This is its best time of year." He left the room to place the vase in the living room, and returned shortly to catch Judy's eye. "Looks great there. I put a bunch like that on the table in my hallway, and the light from the glass panels beside the door hits them in the early morning. Yours will get natural light in the late afternoon."

"You have glass panels by your front door?" Phil asked, surprised. "Isn't that kind of leaving your house vulnerable?"

"They're a stained-glass design of flowers and birds. I love them."

"They're really beautiful," Judy agreed, realizing that this was exactly the kind of thing Phil did that Larry hated. Phil was careful and slightly dogmatic about what the "proper" thing to do was in any given situation.

Phil groaned. "But the chance you're taking! This is San Francisco, Roger. Glass panels are a big temptation to burglars."

Roger's shrug was indifferent. "It's more important to me to live with something beautiful than to spend my life worrying."

"But it's a matter of caution," Phil insisted. "You should see my house. I've got a burglar alarm, and two locks on the front and back doors. I have a timer for the lights to make them go on at different times when I'm working late."

"Well, I lock the doors," Roger admitted. "And the house has never been broken into."

As if he sensed he'd said enough, Phil nodded and said, "You must have a great garden. Those flowers are really something." And their conversation drifted into a discussion of what to plant for foggy weather, and Liza's determination to improve the bare patch of land behind Phil's house.

Judy had finished the dishes and edged toward the kitchen doorway where Roger was standing. He caught hold of her hand and squeezed it warmly. "We really should be off," she said.

"Were you planning to take Larry with you?" Phil asked, his voice sounding almost hopeful.

"Were we?" Roger asked Judy, a mischievous smile tugging at the corners of his mouth.

"No, we weren't," she said firmly.

They were all in the hallway now, and Liza tapped on Larry's door. The teenager appeared after a while, a set of headphones clamped over his ears. When he saw Roger, he smiled, and though his face stiffened almost imperceptibly at the sight of Phil, he very purposefully said, "Hi, Phil. You and Mom going out?"

"Yes. We wondered if you'd like to come to the movie with us," the attorney offered. "It's kind of an arty one at the Bridge. I don't know if you'd like it."

"Oh, thanks for inviting me," Larry said, "but I have plans already. I'm not going to be out late, though, so I can help Mom in the morning with the move."

Judy and Roger exchanged a glance of wry amusement. Larry wished them all a pleasant evening, and, with a friendly wave, disappeared back into his room. Roger squeezed Judy's hand, saying, "We'd better get a move on," and before she could do more than grab her jacket, she found herself hurried down the stairs and out the front door.

"That boy is a quick study," Roger said, grinning widely. "He's going to go places."

"And you can see that Phil's trying, though they both have a way to go."

"Yes, but I'm encouraged. With Liza there to run interference for both of them, with you and me doing what we can, this just might fly." Roger opened the car door for her and kissed her hand before letting it go. "We may have a great future at this."

Chapter Twenty

Roger had warned Judy that he wouldn't be able to see her for a few days. He made brief calls to her each day, but he didn't say much. He didn't run into her in the hospital or the parking garage. It was time that he needed to himself, that period around the first anniversary of Kerri's death.

South of San Francisco was a whole area of cemeteries, as there were really none in the city itself. Roger drove the restored Audi down the 280 freeway and exited at Colma. Through the entrance gates there were rolling green lawns with markers and gravestones strewn across the landscape.

Kerri's ashes were buried here. Roger hadn't wanted them on the mantle in a jar, or scattered at sea. He had wanted to be able to visit them, but not have them in his yard. Kerri had been afraid he might buy some huge, expensive coffin and put a towering stone over her, with angels on it or something. She had made him promise to use restraint, so he had chosen a very simple marker.

Roger drove to the spot he had chosen so carefully and parked the car. He climbed out slowly and moved to stand under the willow-like eucalyptus tree. The small granite stone had only Kerri's name, the dates of her shortened life, and the words "Loved by All." He hadn't been here in two months.

For several minutes Roger stood looking down at the marker. His eyes were dry, but his heart was full. *I know you wanted more than anything for me to be happy, Kerri. And I know you'd want Judy to be happy, too. So I'm going to say good-bye in a different way today. I'll come again, of course, but my life is changing.* I've *changed. I've started living again, and I know you'd be pleased about that. You were a very special person, and I will never for a second regret that you came into my life and that I had that little bit of time with you. Rest in peace, dear one. Forever.*

He ran his fingers along the inscription on the stone, sighed, and turned his face up to the sun lacing its way through the graceful branches.

Judy had been slightly alarmed by Roger's uncharacteristic uncommunicativeness. She hadn't seen him for several days when he appeared on the oncology floor at the end of her shift. He looked different somehow.

"Is everything okay?" she asked, automatically reaching out to touch his arm.

"Yes," he said. "We need to talk. I thought maybe we could walk along the path by the ocean."

She agreed to go, though she felt a heart-pounding fear that he was going to tell her he couldn't handle this after all, that she was a perfectly wonderful woman but he wasn't ready for a perfectly wonderful woman in his life.

Still, he held her hand as they walked through the hospital corridors, and in the elevator, and out the front entrance. He held it as they crossed the grassy stretches of the Fielding Medical Center campus. The trail he had selected led along the ridge overlooking the ocean, the Golden Gate Bridge and the hills of Marin.

Judy's gaze strayed from the spectacular scenery to Roger's face. "I'll find a way to handle it if you're still in love with Kerri, Roger. I'll understand if this is all too much too soon."

Roger squeezed her hand and smiled. "I loved Kerri, and I was proud that she agreed to marry me. I knew, of course, that she was dying, though sometimes I wouldn't admit it, even to myself. She was sick most of the time I knew her, but there were some good months when she seemed healthy. She was a super person."

"I don't think I've ever met anyone quite so lovable, so full of kindness and generosity of spirit. She was a remarkable woman."

Roger nodded. "What we had wasn't quite what other people have. It was different because it was so precarious. It was intense because it was so short. From the day I met her before her original surgery, there was that threat hanging over her life. She became very precious to me. I knew, I think, from the very beginning, that I would lose her, that I would have to let her go."

He turned to face Judy fully, gripping both of her hands in his. "But now, I've let her go, Judy, because I've fallen in love with you. You're the woman I love, the woman who fills my mind and my heart to bursting. I'll always love Kerri, but not in the same way. I didn't think that would ever change. I didn't think it could. I thought I would love her the same way always. That was pretty naive of me, I suppose, but that's how it felt when she died."

Judy felt surprisingly breathless. "I think she'd understand, Roger. But are you sure you love me? Are you sure it's not just the relief of opening up to the world again, and finding me there on your path?"

He grinned. "Oh, yes, I'm quite sure. Because I didn't feel this way about Kerri, you see. She was like a goddess, so fragile because of her health, and so otherworldly in her goodness. I worshiped her. I don't worship you."

"Thank God!" Judy said, but she felt shaky, too.

She had thought herself altogether too human, too real for someone to fall in love with.

Roger let out a long, sighing breath. "You and I are much better suited than Kerri and I were, and what I feel about you is all the more potent because of it. I was always afraid Kerri would discover my feet of clay, that I would let her down. You already know who I really am, and you seem to accept me anyhow."

She touched his dear face with tender fingers. "That's one of the things that makes me love you, that you're so frank and so earnest. You don't always think you're right, and you don't always do the accepted thing. I love your eagerness, and your curiosity, and your humor."

She stood on tiptoe to kiss his forehead. "When I'm with you, I'm beginning to trust that I don't have to be perfect, I just have to be me."

His eyes, unshaded from the August sun, gleamed with mischief. "Where's the fun in being perfect? Life's much more interesting when you have people like Larry challenging your ingenuity to find the best in them. And I feel sure we can find the best in each other just by being together."

He motioned toward the misted Marin hills and the glowing towers of the bridge. "This is the ideal spot, obviously. But does it seem too soon for me to propose to you?"

"We don't have to make this something permanent yet, Roger. There's plenty of time."

"I know that. But I know this is something I want now. I hope you do, too. I want us to have kids before we get too old to run around with them, and I want us to live together in the house on Cherry Street. Because it was never really Kerri's house. She was so sick when she came there that she wasn't able to make an imprint on it. Maybe that's why I tried so hard to fill it with pictures of her.

"But we don't *have* to stay there, if it would bother you. We could sell it and get a different house, one we picked out together. It doesn't matter as much to me as just living somewhere with you." He brought her hands up to his lips and kissed them. "So what do you say, love? Will you marry me?"

"There's nothing I'd rather do," she admitted, laughter bubbling up from the release of her anxiety. "But you may be forgetting that you're letting yourself in for Larry and Liza and Phil, too. Nobody comes without baggage, do they?"

"Nope. I've watched them all—Angel and Cliff, Rachel and Jerry, Nan and Steve. They bring along the most incredible baggage. What it does is make their relationships richer, like dragging along a treasure chest, filled with the sad and wonderful stuff of life. We'll have ours, too, and we'll keep adding to it as we go along. That's the way life is."

Roger folded her in his arms. Judy snuggled

against him, raising her face for his soft and eager kiss. This was not what she had expected to happen, and yet it seemed perfectly right. She sighed and whispered in his ear, “Let's go home.”